# Progressive
# First
# Flute Book

## by
## Andrew Scott

# You Learn Faster When You Know How It Should Sound

All the exercises and songs in Progressive First Flute Book have been recorded onto a stereo cassette or CD, which enables you to hear what you should be playing. This is a valuable method for learning quickly, and it also makes practicing more enjoyable, as you can play along with professional musicians from your very first lesson.

Each exercise has been recorded in stereo to enable you to listen to and play along with either:

1.  the flute by itself
    (balance control fully to the left), or

2.  the flute with the backing instruments
    (balance control in the centre position), or

3.  the backing instruments only
    (balance control fully to the right).

A drum is used to begin each exercise and to help you keep in time.

**Acknowledgements**

Photos by Phil Martin
Diagrams and illustrations by James Stewart
Cover instrument supplied by Allans Music

**ISBN 0 947183 52 3**
**SET 0 947183 53 1**

Reorder Code KP-F

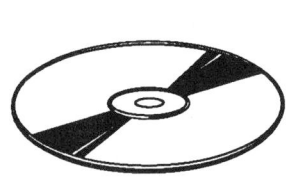

# Contents

**Contents continued on next page**

4

## Contents (continued)

# Introduction

Progressive First Flute Book has been designed to introduce the student to the basics of flute playing and reading music.

To maximise the student's enjoyment and interest, the book incorporates an extensive repertoire of well-known songs. All the songs and exercises have been carefully graded into an easy-to-follow, lesson-by-lesson format, which assumes no prior knowledge of music or the flute by the student. Chord symbols for guitar and piano accompaniment are provided for each song and exercise.

This book incorporates very easy arrangements involving twelve natural notes, two sharp notes and one flat note. It introduces $\frac{4}{4}$ and $\frac{3}{4}$ time, whole, half, quarter, and eighth notes and their equivalent rests, and describes in detail the correct procedure for breathing and blowing efficiency.

The student is taught how to read music, and introduced to basic terms such as bar lines, repeat signs and lead-in notes. The glossary of musical terms is provided for students to expand their musical knowledge, and the fingering index extends the range of notes to cover two octaves.

# Lesson 1
## How to Assemble the Flute

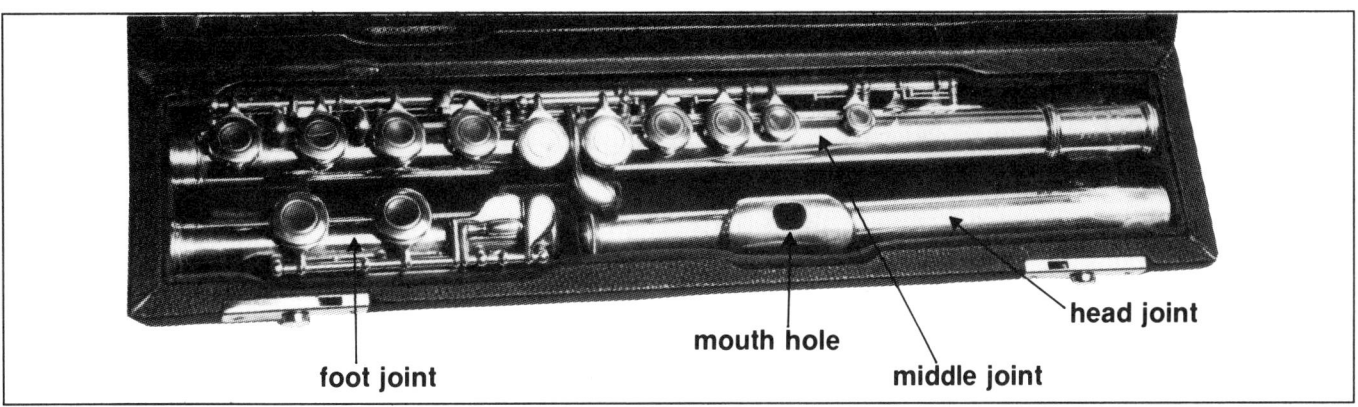

foot joint      mouth hole      middle joint      head joint

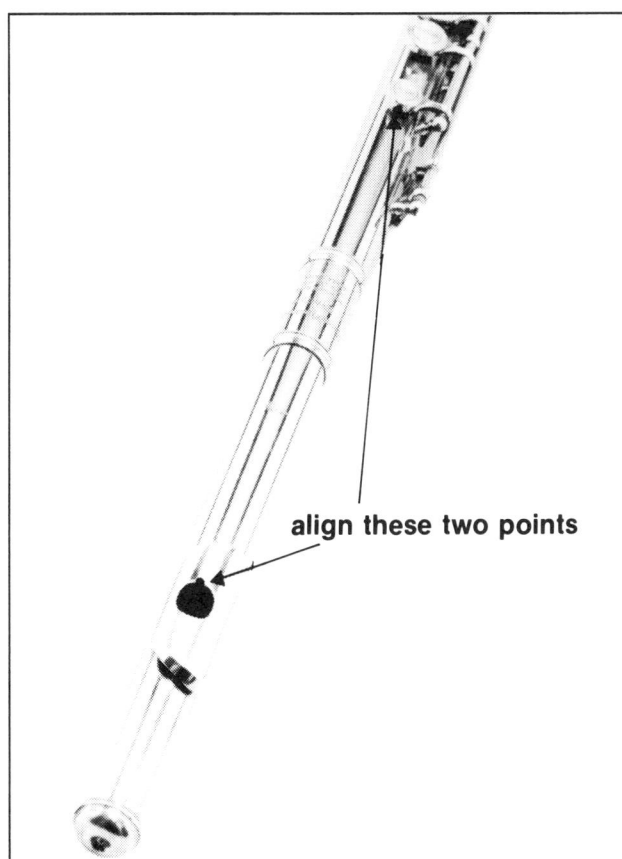

align these two points

Find all the parts of the flute that are shown in photo 1.

Insert the head joint into the middle joint with a twisting motion. Align the mouth hole with the key on the middle joint as shown in photo 2.

Attach the foot joint to the middle joint. Rotate it so that the middle of the first lever on the foot joint is opposite the end of the shaft on the middle joint, as shown in photo 3.

These positions are only approximate. You may want to adjust them after you have become more familiar with the flute.

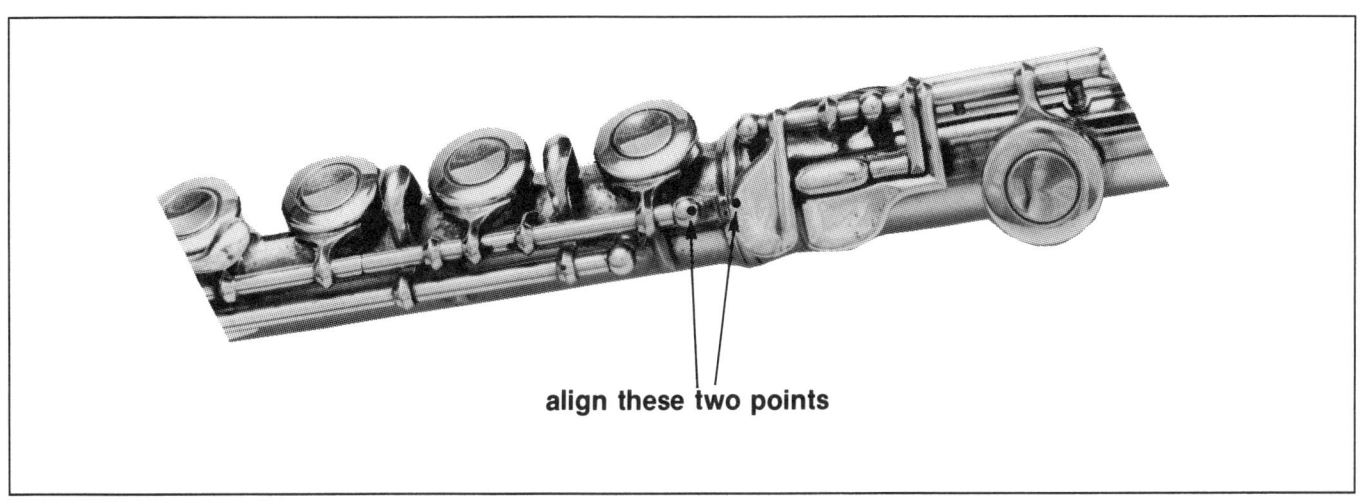

align these two points

# How to Hold the Flute

Have the palm of your **left** hand facing **towards** you, and the palm of your **right** hand facing **away** from you. Put your fingers in position for the note G, as shown in the diagram below. You should support the flute in four places –

1. the mouthpiece should be held firm against your lower lip;

2. the first finger of your left hand (between the hand and the first knuckle) supports the body of the flute;

3. with your right thumb, placed below your first or second fingers;

4. your right hand fourth finger has a negligible effect on the sound of many notes, but acts as a counterbalance to the other points of support.

**Right Hand**

**Left Hand**

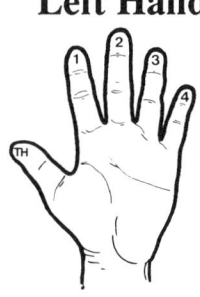

The numbers on the fingers correspond to the numbers on the diagram below.

# Flute ④ Fingering Diagram

**Left Hand Fingers**                              **Right Hand Fingers**

A white number or letter in a black key means that you hold the key down with the finger indicated.

A black number or letter in a white key means that you let the tip of your finger or thumb hover near the key, ready to play a different note.

When your fingers are in the positions indicated here, you are fingering the note G. On your flute there are two positions for your left thumb. Make sure that your thumb only touches the part of the flute marked TH on the diagram.

# How to Make a Sound

Put your fingers in position for the note G, and hold the mouthpiece of the flute against your lower lip so that your lip covers about one quarter of the hole.

Blow **across** the hole towards the centre of the opposite edge. If the flute makes a sound, you are doing everything right.

If you can't make a sound, it may be necessary to do a lot of experimenting. Try moving the flute to the left or the right, or roll it towards or away from you. The note will only sound in a very precise place, so only move the flute a little at a time. Blow with smooth, sustained breaths, rather than short puffs.

If nothing happens except that you get dizzy, don't worry. The flute is the most difficult wind instrument to begin learning. Anyone can sit down at a piano and play a note immediately. There is no

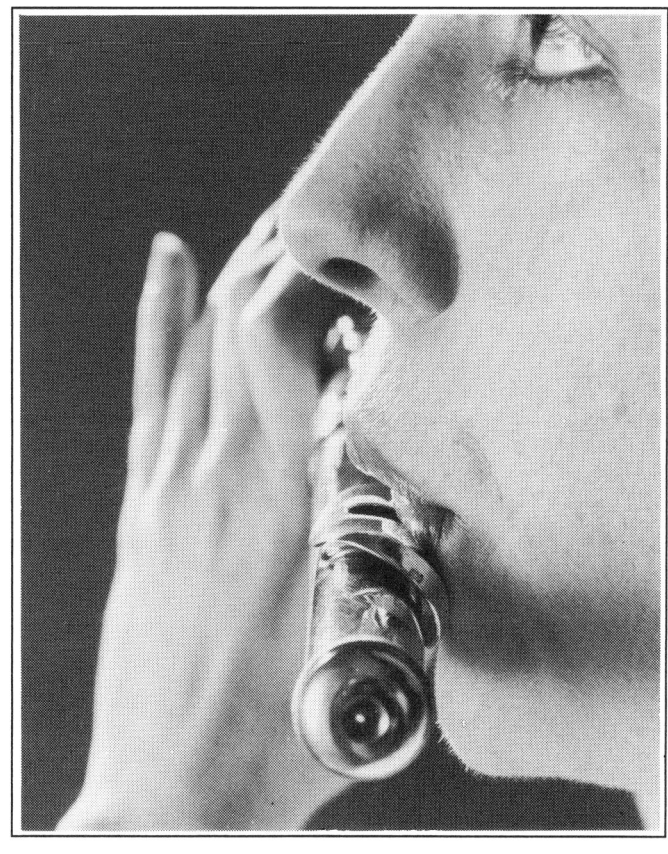

effort involved in making the instrument produce a sound. Playing a note on the flute is a much more complicated process, so don't be disappointed if it takes many hours of practice before you can make a note clearly.

When you have succeeded in making a sound, try to be aware of the sensation in your lips. Associate the sensation with the sound, and aim to recreate the sensation to recreate the sound.

# Tonguing

The notes will have a definite start and finish if you use a technique known as **tonguing**. Without the flute, say the word "**too**". Say it in a whisper. Notice that your tongue starts at the back of your top teeth, and you make the "too" sound by quickly withdrawing it, a little like spitting.

Say "too" again in a whisper, and this time follow through with your breath, so that you create a continuous air stream. This is how you should start a note when you play the flute. Now with the flute against your lip, hold your tongue against your top teeth, as you build up pressure in your mouth. Quickly release your tongue, and the note should start, definitely and crisply. To stop the note, simply replace your tongue against your teeth. The note will stop immediately, and your tongue will be in a position to start the next note.

# Lesson 2
# How to Tune Your Flute to the Cassette

1. Adjust the headjoint of your flute so that it is pulled out from the middle joint approximately one quarter of an inch (six millimetres).

2. Play your G note.

3. Start the cassette and listen to the note that occurs at the beginning.

4. If the note on the cassette sounds the same as your note, you are **in tune**. Proceed to the next page.

5. If the note on the cassette sounds **higher** (**sharper**) than your note, your flute is **flat**. You will need to make it sharper by pushing the headjoint into the middle joint a little more (about one sixteenth of an inch - two mm). Use a twisting motion as you do this, and be careful not to alter the alignment of the mouth hole with the body of the flute. Play your G again, then compare it with the cassette. Keep doing this until your G note sounds the same as the cassette. If the head joint is all the way in the flute still sounds flat, turn the headjoint away from you a little. This will raise the pitch a bit more.

6. If the note on the cassette sounds **lower** (**flatter**) than your note, your flute is **sharp**. You will need to make it flatter by pulling the headjoint out of the middle joint a little more (about one sixteenth of an inch - two mm). Play your G again, then compare it with the cassette. Keep doing this until your G note sounds the same as the cassette.

7. As a final check, play your G at the same time as the note on the cassette. If they are in tune, they will sound like one instrument. If not, there will be an unpleasant beating sound. Return to step 2.

## Summary

To make the flute sound **SH**arper (Higher), make it **SH**orter.

To make the flute sound f**L**atter (Lower), make it **L**onger.

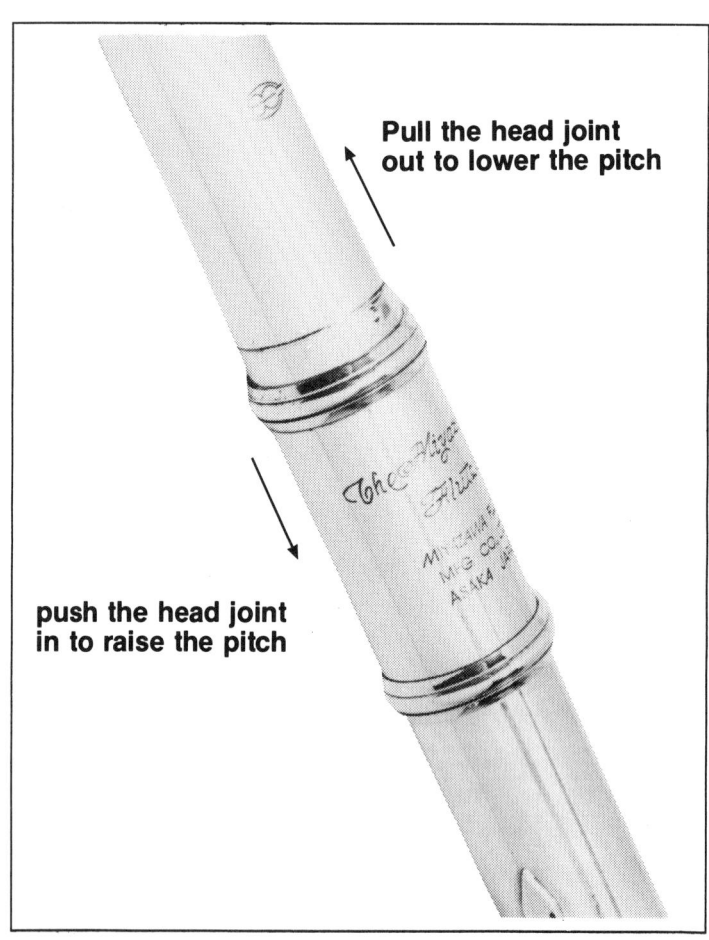

**Pull the head joint out to lower the pitch**

**push the head joint in to raise the pitch**

# How to Read Music

There are only seven letters used for notes in music. They are:

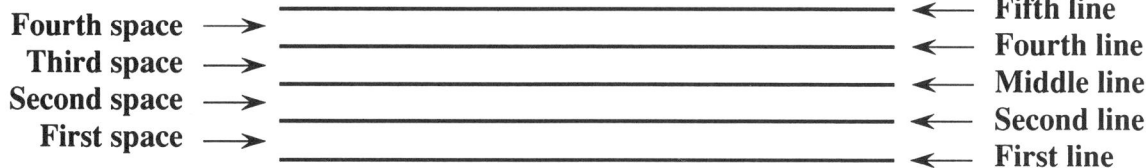

A   B   C   D   E   F   G

These notes are known as the **musical alphabet**.

# The Staff

These five lines are called the **staff** or **stave**.

Fourth space →
Third space →
Second space →
First space →

← Fifth line
← Fourth line
← Middle line
← Second line
← First line

## The Treble Clef

This symbol is called a **treble clef**. It dictates the position of notes on the staff.

There is a treble clef at the start of every line of flute music.

# The Half Note

This is a music note called a **half note** (or **minim**). It has a value of **two** beats.

Count **1** 2

# The Note G

Music notes are written in the spaces and on the lines of the staff. This note is a G note. It is written on the **second** line of the staff.

# Bars

Music is divided into **bars** (or **measures**) by **bar lines**.

1 bar

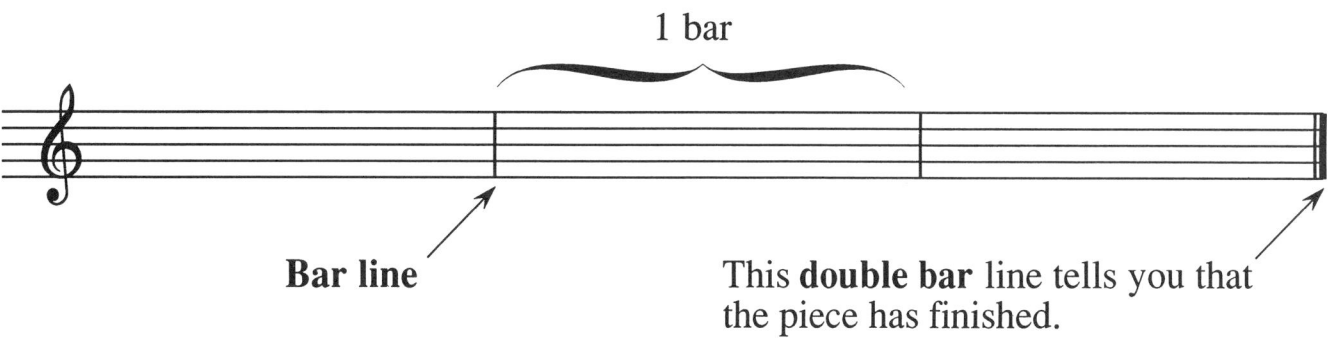

**Bar line**

This **double bar** line tells you that the piece has finished.

# The Four Four Time Signature

**4/4** These two numbers are called a **time signature**. They are placed after the treble clef.

The $\frac{4}{4}$ time signature tells you that there are **four** beats in each bar.

## 📼 Exercise 1

To play Exercise 1, count up to four before starting, to get the feel of the rhythm.

Think — **one two** as you play the first G in each bar.

— **three four** as you play the second G in each bar.

Tap your foot if it helps you count the beats.

Take a breath where you see this mark: ▼

On the cassette there are **four** drumbeats to introduce exercises in $\frac{4}{4}$ time.

The letters above the staff are chord symbols, and are played by accompanying instruments, e.g. piano or guitar.

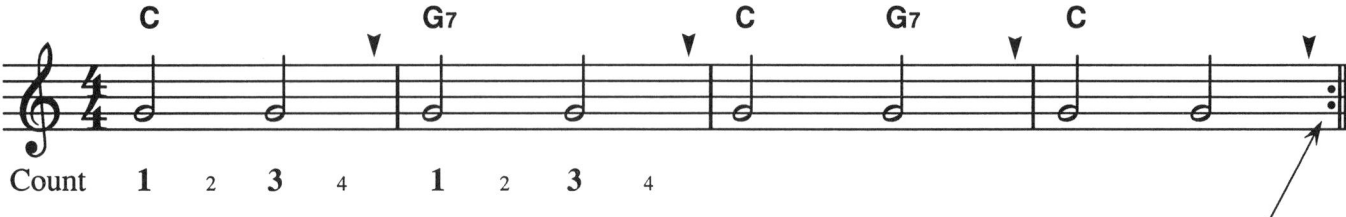

Count 1 2 3 4 1 2 3 4

The big numbers **1** and **3** tell you to play the note. The small numbers 2 and 4 tell you to sustain it until the next note. Notice that there are four beats in each bar.

These two dots are called a **repeat sign**. This means that you play the exercise again from the start.

Count 1 2

# The Half Rest

This black box is called a **half rest**, (or **minim rest**). It means **two** beats of silence. To play this rest, count for **two beats** without playing any note.

## 📼 Exercise 2

Count 1 2 3 4 1 2 3 4

Small counting numbers are used under rests.

## 📼 Exercise 3

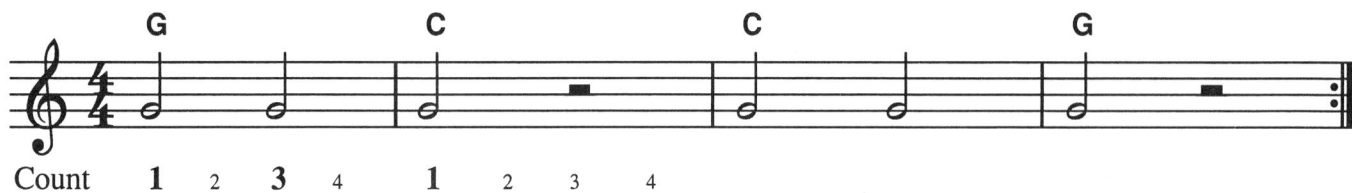

Count 1 2 3 4 1 2 3 4

# The Quarter Note

This symbol is called a **quarter note** (or **crotchet**). It means play the note for **one** beat. Make sure you tongue each note.

Count **1**

## 🎵 Exercise 4

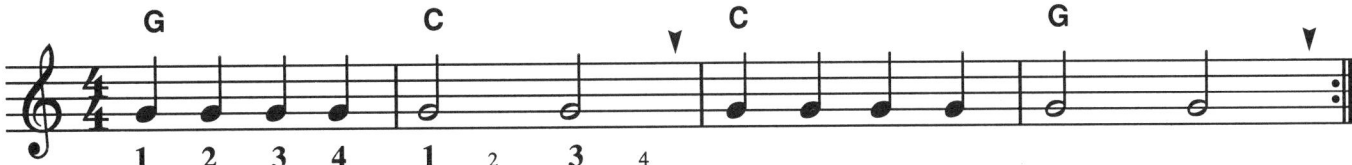

## 🎵 Tongue Tied

Quarter notes and half notes can be combined in a bar so that each bar has a total of **four** beats.

Only one bar line means continue to the next line of music.

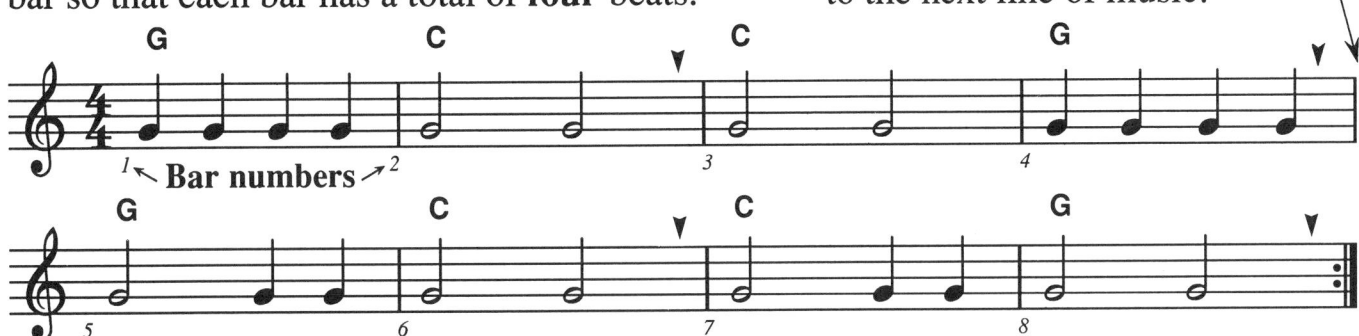

# The Quarter Rest

This symbol is a **quarter rest** (or **crotchet rest**). It means one beat of silence. To play this rest, count for one beat without playing a note.

Count 1

## 🎵 Exercise 5

## 🎵 Rest Easy

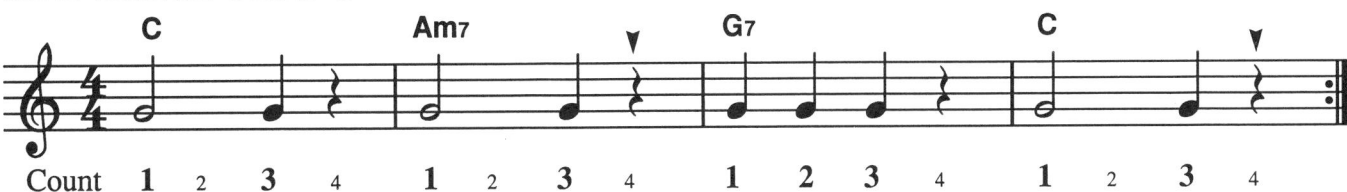

# Lesson 3
## The Note A

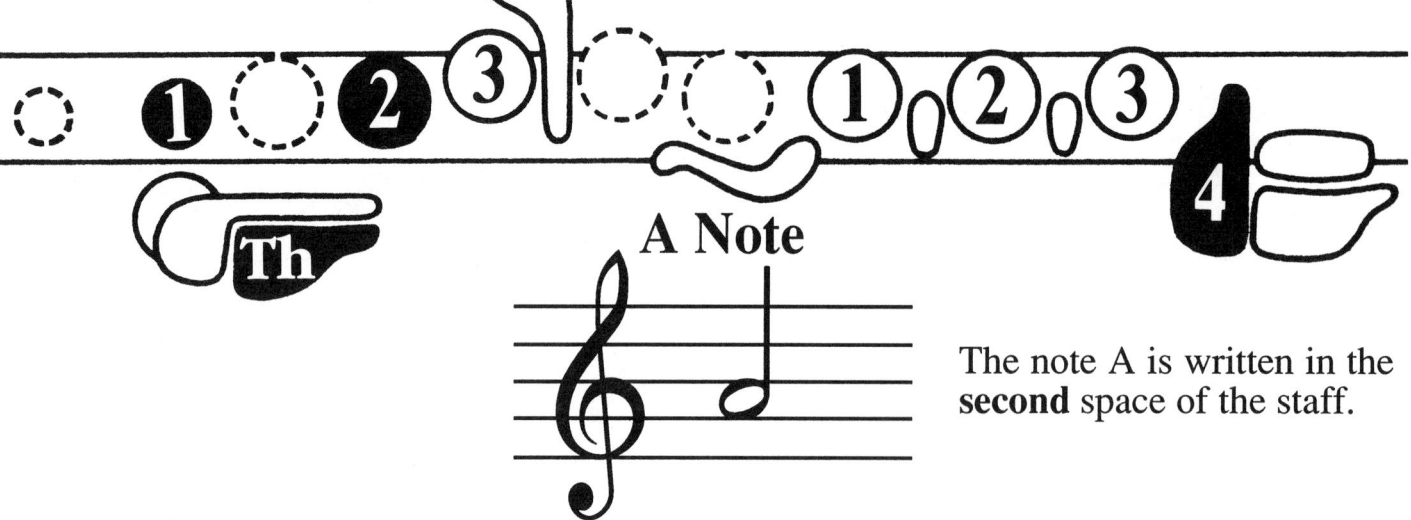

### A Note

The note A is written in the **second** space of the staff.

## 🔊 Take the A-Plane

## 🔊 Two Note Samba

In this song you use the two notes you have learnt so far. The first and second fingers of your left hand stay on the keys for both notes. Lift your third finger off to change from G to A.

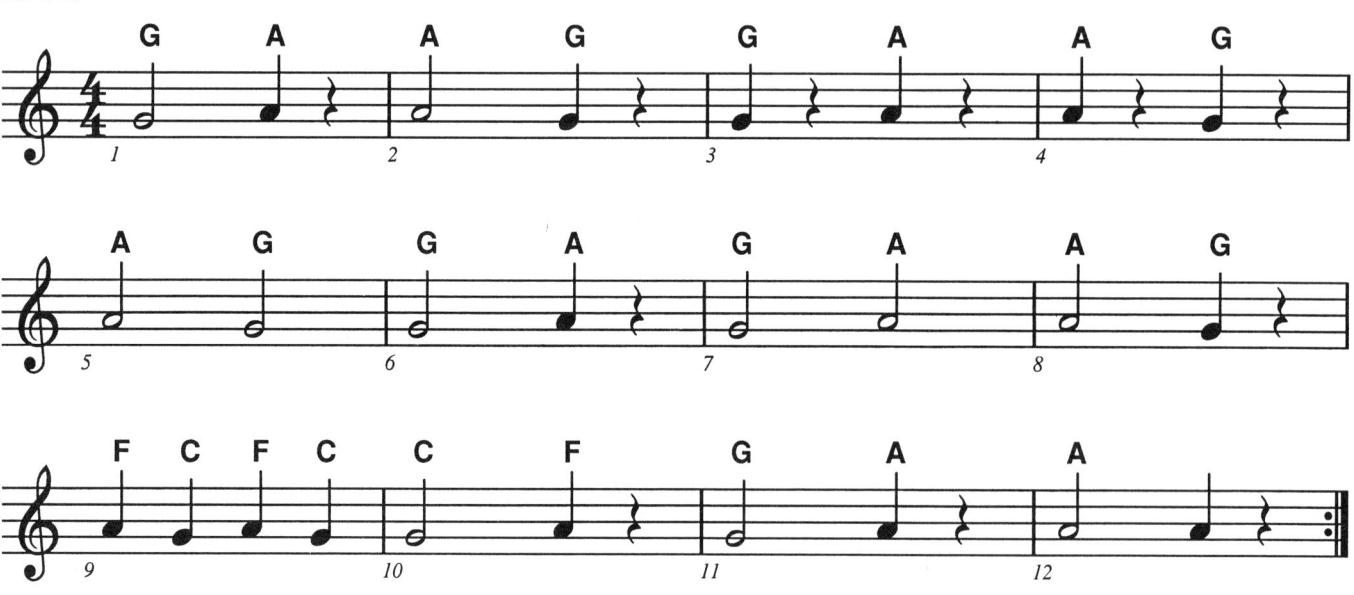

# The Galway Piper

Traditional

This song is a **duet** – a piece for two instruments. The student plays the top line and the teacher plays the bottom line. Practice playing your part along with the teacher's part on the cassette.

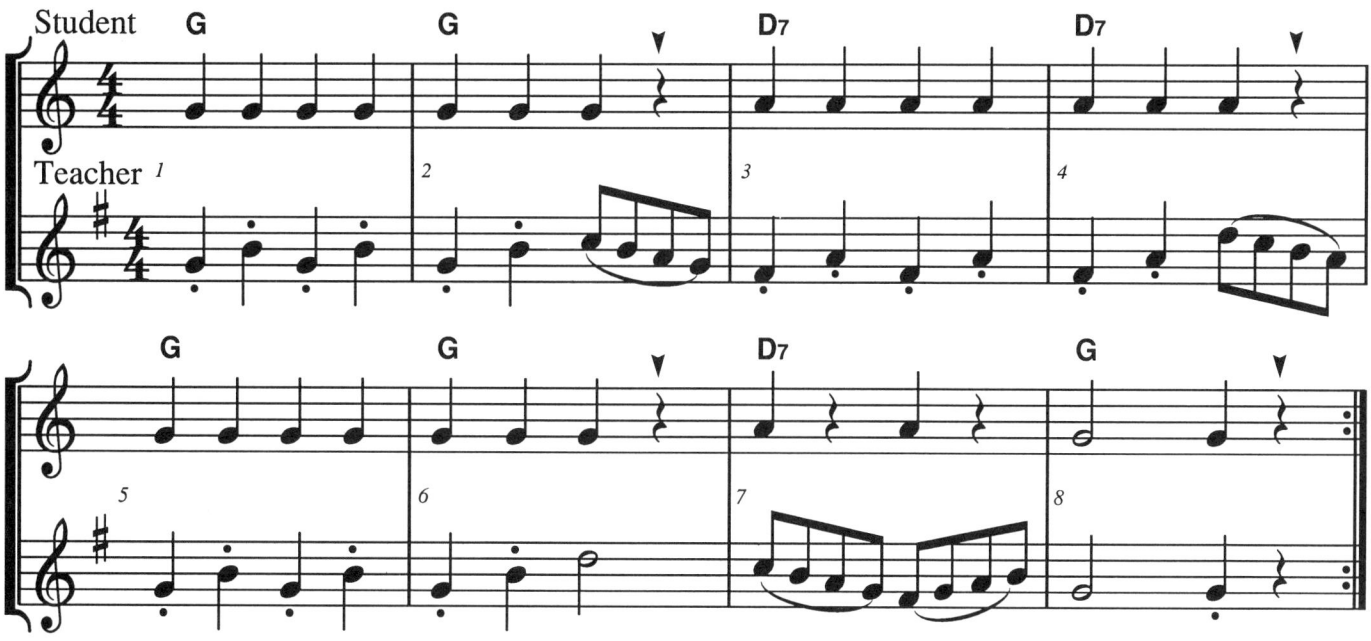

# Two Blue

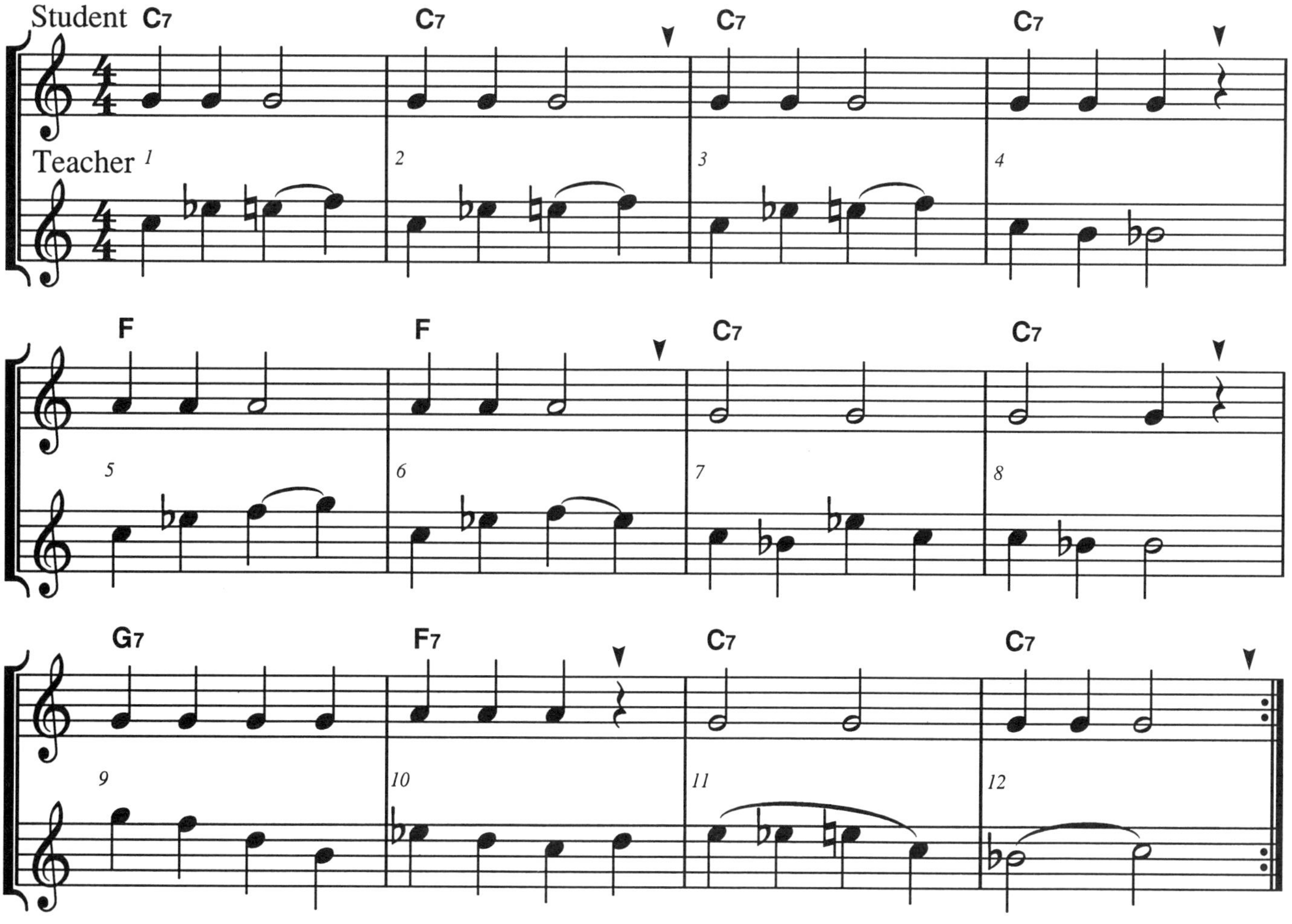

# The Note B

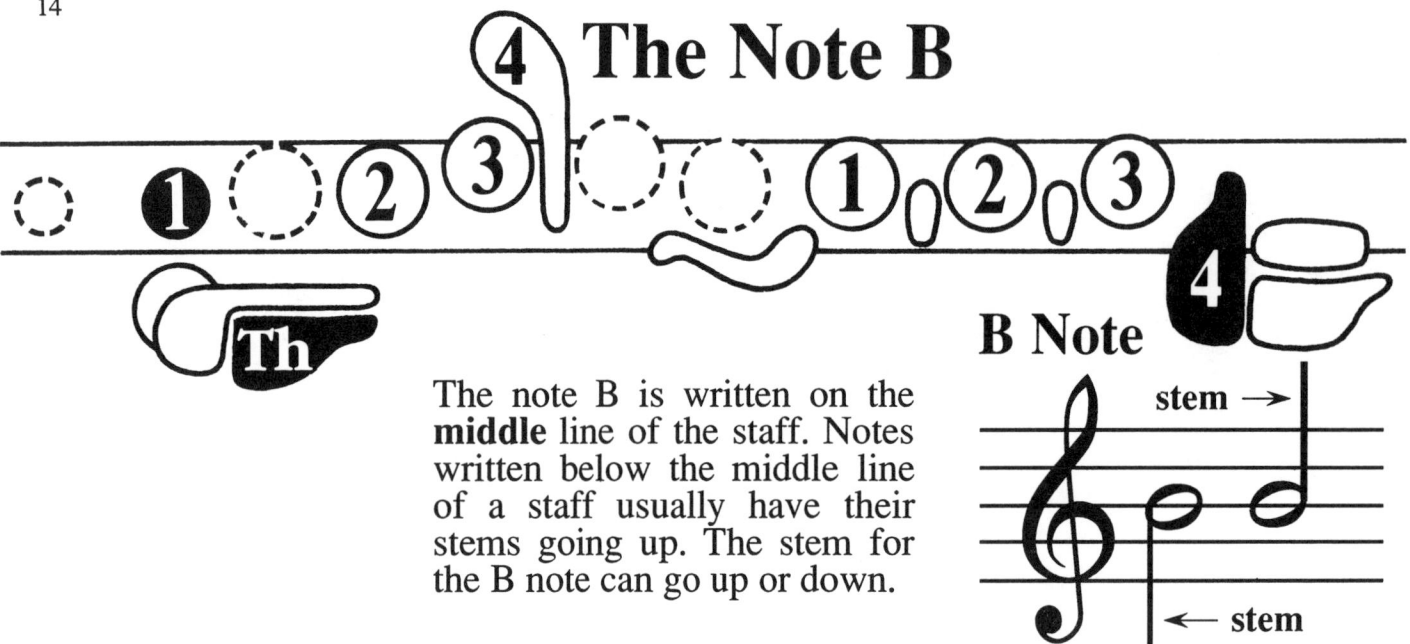

The note B is written on the **middle** line of the staff. Notes written below the middle line of a staff usually have their stems going up. The stem for the B note can go up or down.

B Note

stem →

← stem

To make the B note sound clear, make sure you have your left thumb only on the key marked TH and not the key next to it.

## B-Ware

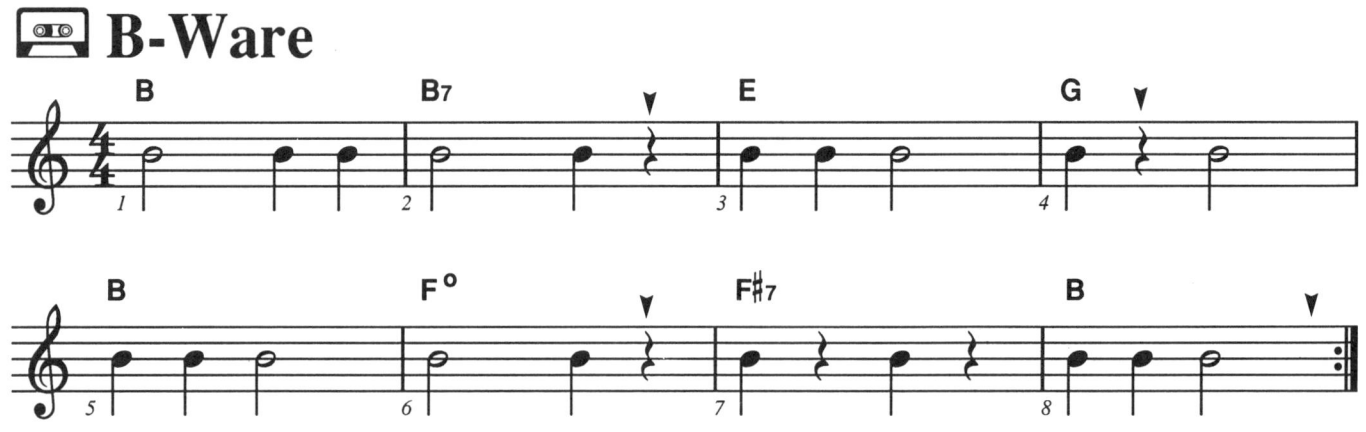

If you have trouble distinguishing the notes from each other, write their names below the staff, as in Exercise 6.

## Exercise 6

## Exercise 7

## 🔊 Mixed Bag

## 🔊 Rock Solid

# Health Hints

Most people experience cramps in their little finger from continuously holding open the key on the foot joint, arm pains from supporting the flute, and dizziness from all the blowing. These conditions are only temporary, and will disappear with practice, especially after you learn the Effortless Breathing Technique in Lesson 8.

# Lesson 4
## The Note C

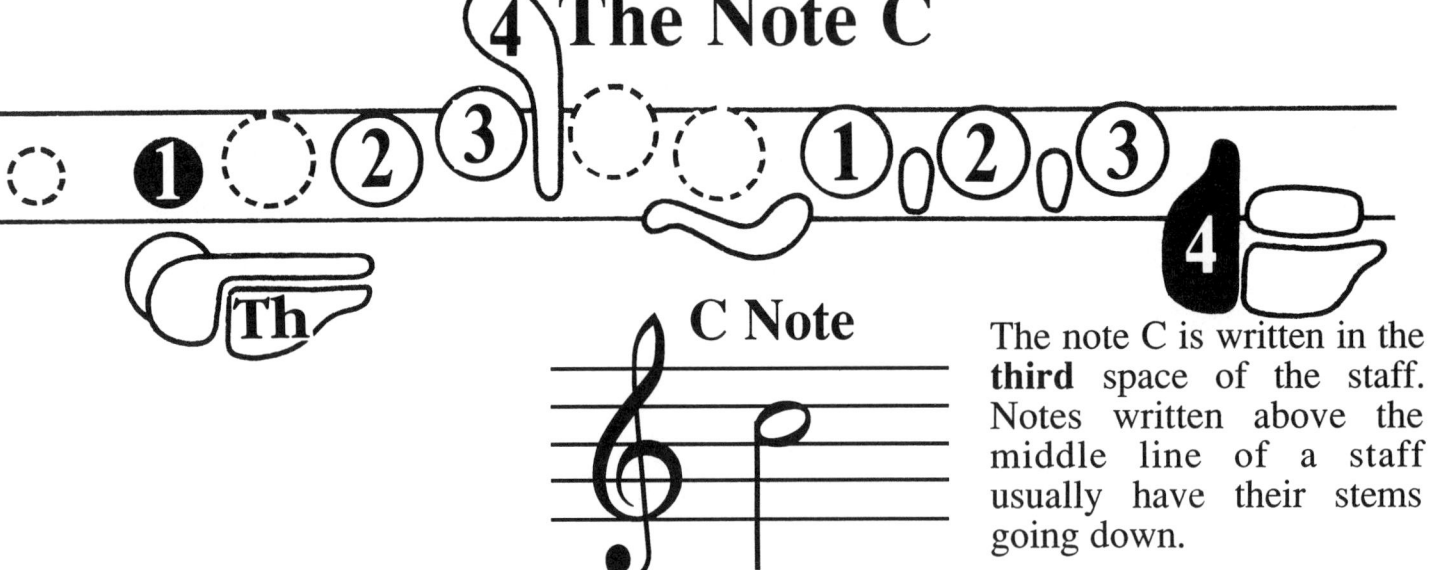

### C Note

The note C is written in the **third** space of the staff. Notes written above the middle line of a staff usually have their stems going down.

You may feel that the flute is difficult to balance when you finger this note. Make sure that the lower part of your left hand first finger is pressing against the tube. Try to avoid resting your left thumb on the flute, as you will need to have it near its key to play other notes. It will become easier to play C as you grow more familiar with the flute.

## Exercise 8

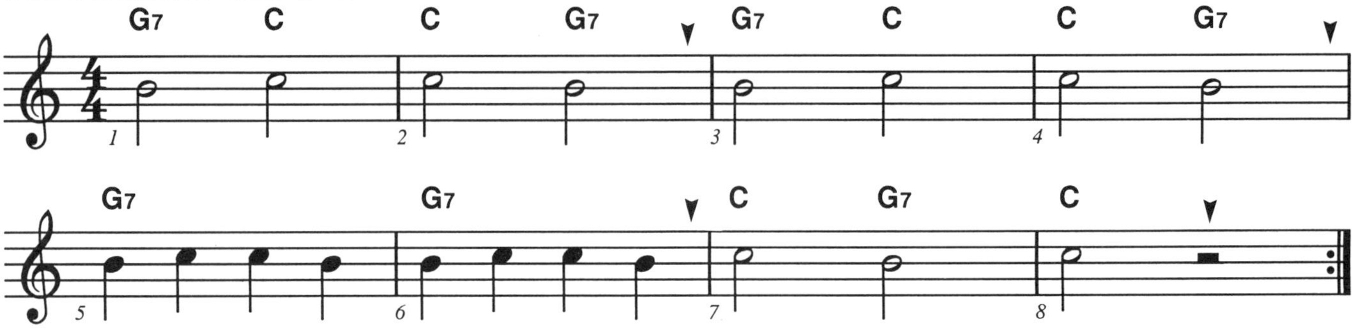

## Exercise 9

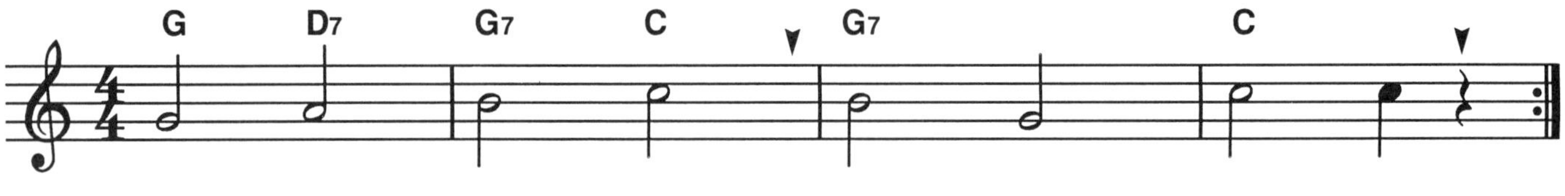

## Easy to C

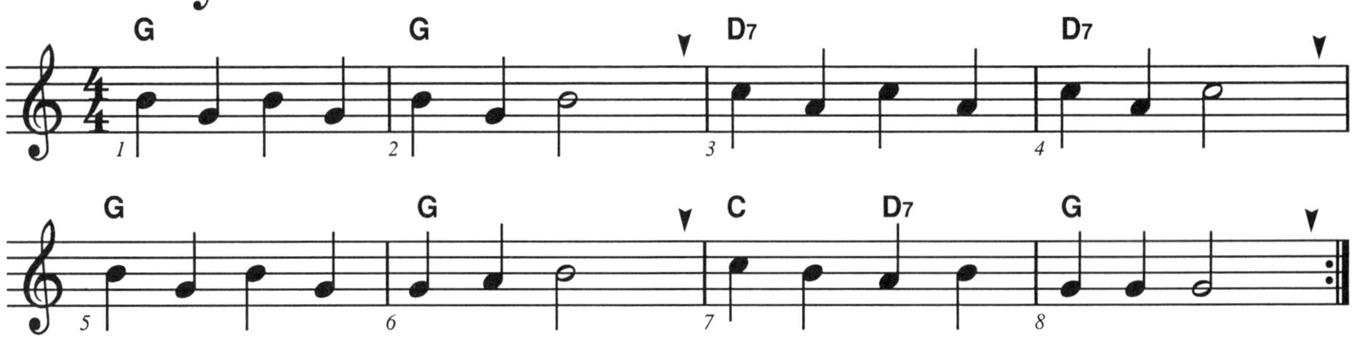

# The Dotted Half Note

A **dot** written after a note lengthens its value by a half. A dot placed after a half note means that you hold the note for **three** beats.

1 beat
quarter note

2 beats
half note

3 beats
dotted half note

## Crystal Rock

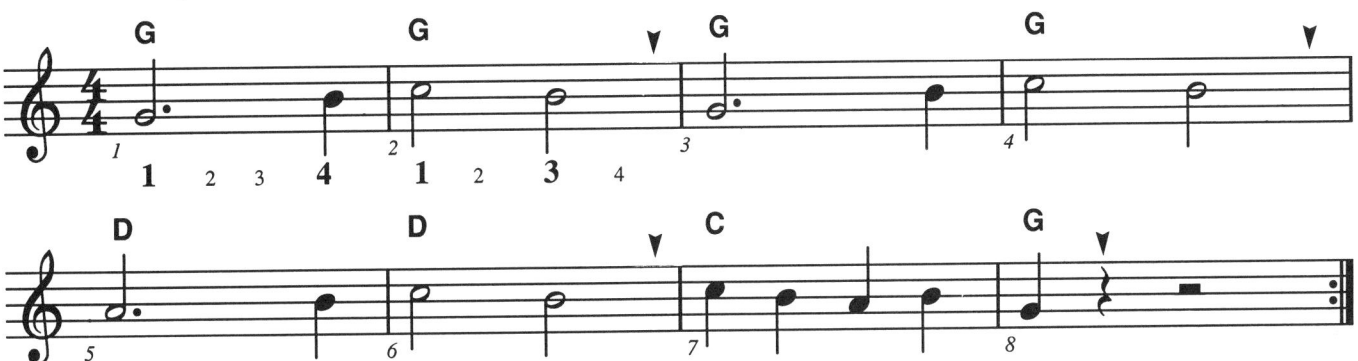

## Mango Tango

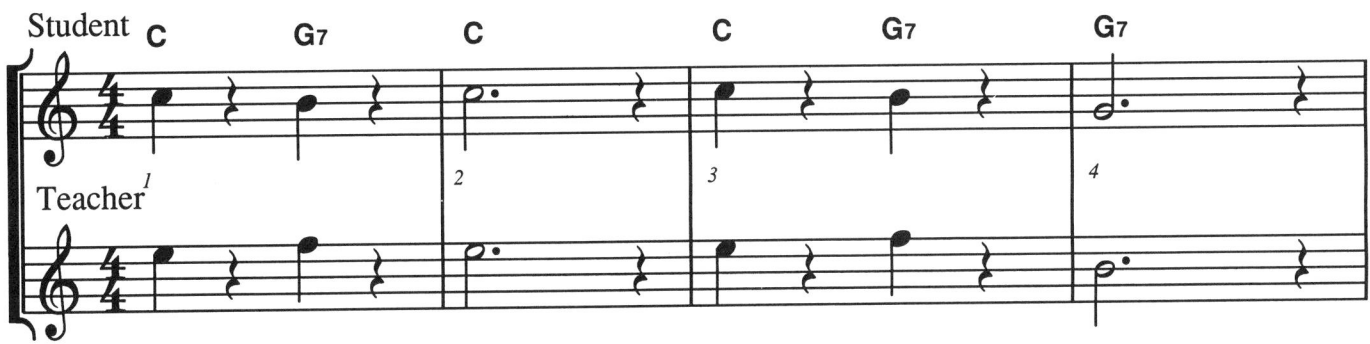

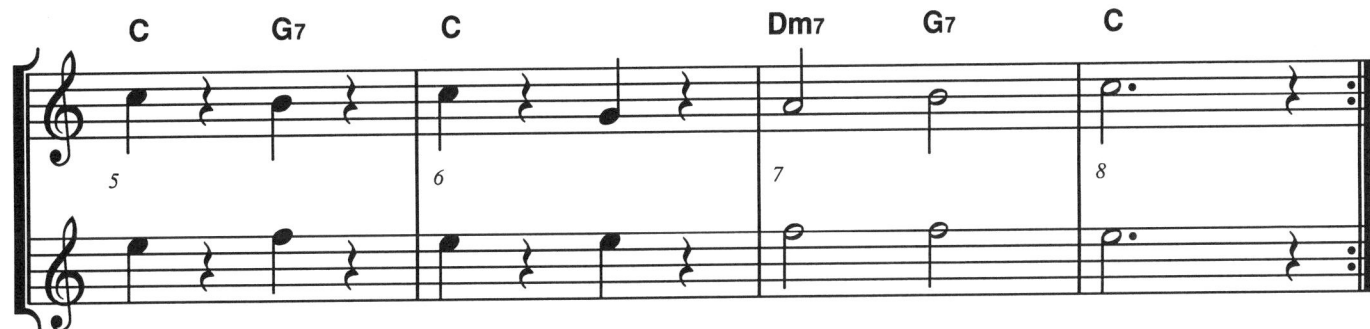

# The Three Four Time Signature

The $\frac{3}{4}$ after the treble clef means that there are only **three** beats in each bar. This gives the rhythm a completely different feel to $\frac{4}{4}$ time.

$\frac{3}{4}$ is also known as **waltz** time.

## Three's a Crowd

On the cassette there are **three** drumbeats to introduce songs in $\frac{3}{4}$ time.

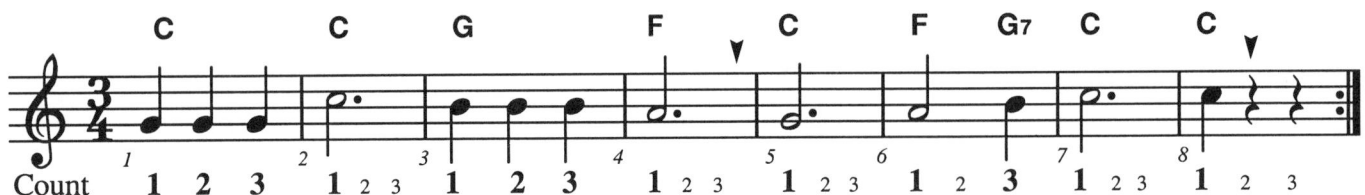

## Barcarolle

Jacques Offenbach

## Opera House Waltz

# Lesson 5
## The Note F

**F Note**

The note F is written in the **first** space of the staff.

 ## Exercise 10

F          F          B♭          F

 ## Autumn's Theme

Student    C          F          G          G

Teacher

F          F          G7          C

# The Slur

## 📼 Exercise 11

Tongue only the **first** note.

The **slur** is a curved line drawn above (or below) two or more different notes. It tells you to play the notes smoothly. Playing smoothly is called **legato**. To play the notes smoothly, only tongue the first note of the group and keep blowing while you change your fingers.

## 📼 To Slur with Love

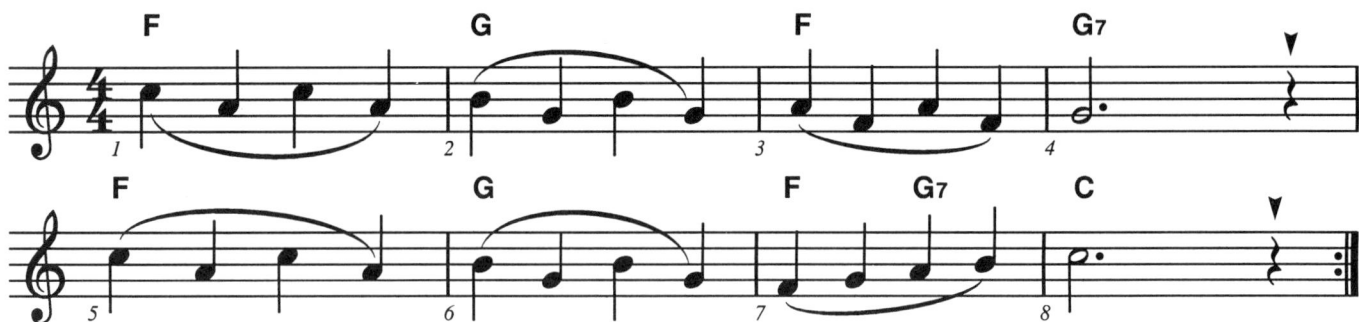

## 📼 Orange Blossom

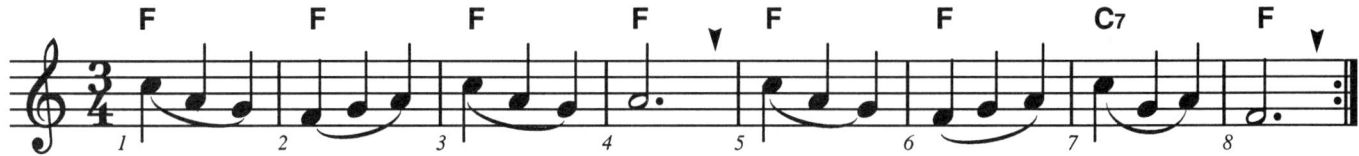

# Staccato

## 📼 Exercise 12

A dot placed above or below a note tells you to play the note **staccato**. Staccato means to play a note short and separate from other notes. To play a note short, make a "t" action with your tongue, instead of the longer "too" action.

Staccato is the opposite of legato.

## 📼 CC Senor

This song combines staccato and legato.

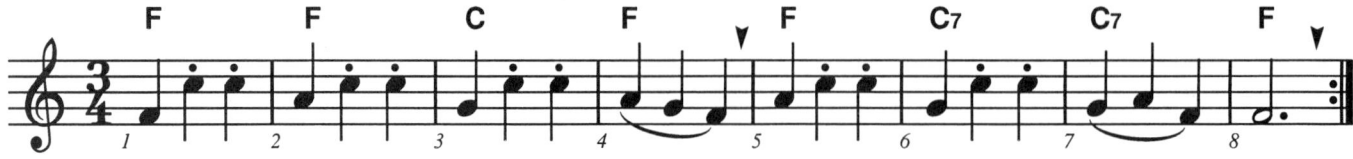

# Flat Signs

This is a **flat** sign.

A flat sign lowers the pitch of the note to which it applies by an **interval** (see glossary) known as one **semitone** (or one **half step**). Thus the note B♭ is one semitone **lower** than B. Since the difference in pitch between the notes A and B is one whole tone (two semitones), B♭ is also one semitone **higher** than A.

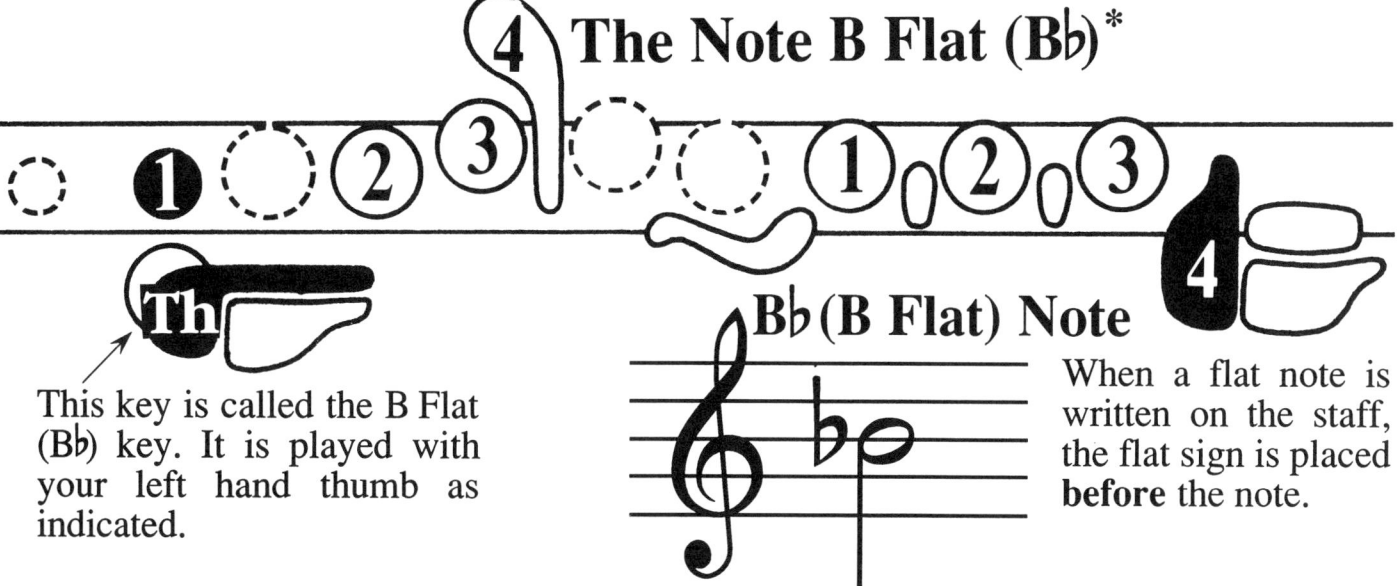

## The Note B Flat (B♭)*

This key is called the B Flat (B♭) key. It is played with your left hand thumb as indicated.

### B♭ (B Flat) Note

When a flat note is written on the staff, the flat sign is placed **before** the note.

Notice that your thumb can remain on the B♭ key while you play many notes without their being affected. This is because the B♭ key is connected to the key between fingers 1 and 2 on the left hand. That key is closed for all notes below and including A.

## Exercise 13

Place your thumb on the B♭ key before you play this exercise.

## Ode to Joy

Ludwig van Beethoven

Instead of writing a flat sign before every B♭ note, it is easier to write just one flat sign after the treble clef. This means that all B notes on the staff are played as B♭, even though there is no flat sign placed before the note.

Thumb on B♭ key.

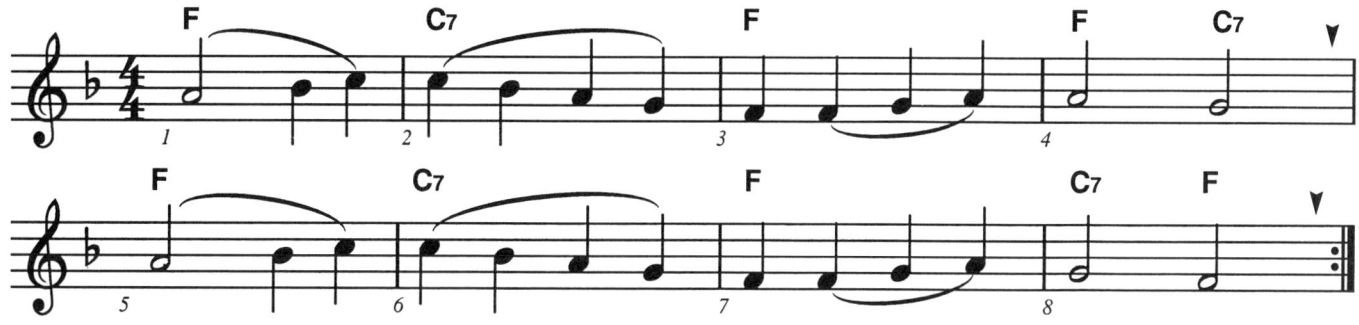

*Consult the index of fingerings for an alternative method of playing B♭.

# Lesson 6

## The Common Time Signature

**C** This symbol is called **common time**.
It means exactly the same as $\frac{4}{4}$ time.

###  Mambo Jumbo

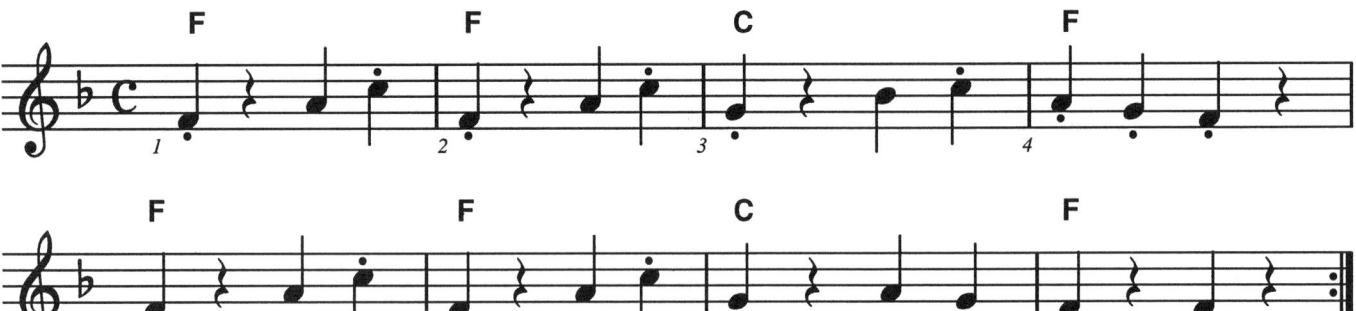

###  Aura Lee

Traditional

Thumb on B♭ key.

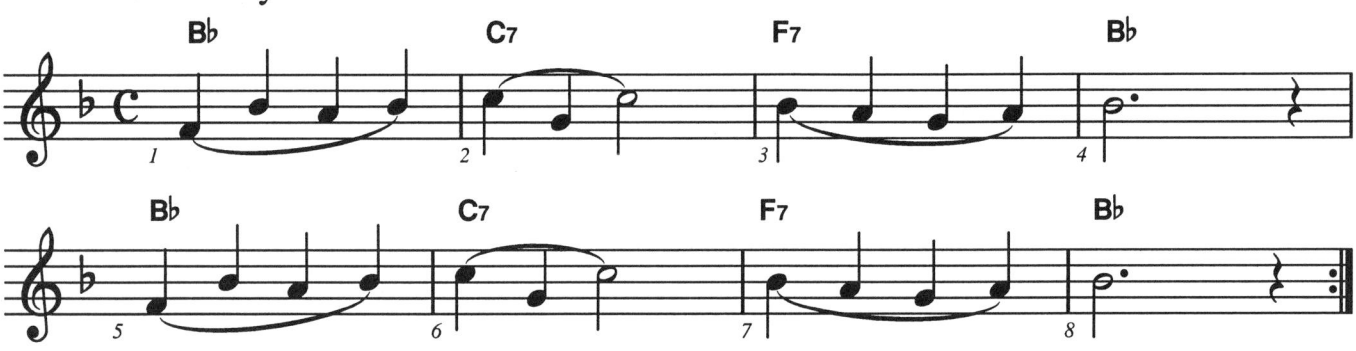

### Austrian Waltz

Traditional Austrian

# The Tie

## 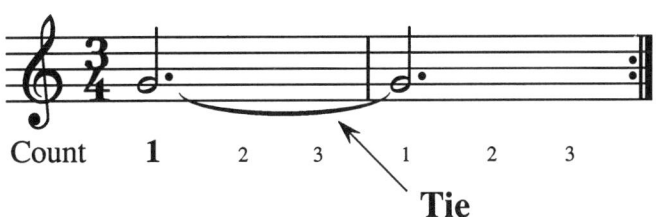 Exercise 14

A **tie** is a curved line that connects two notes with the same position on the staff. The tie tells you to tongue the first note only, and to hold it for the length of both notes.

## Beautiful Brown Eyes

Traditional

Thumb on B♭ key.

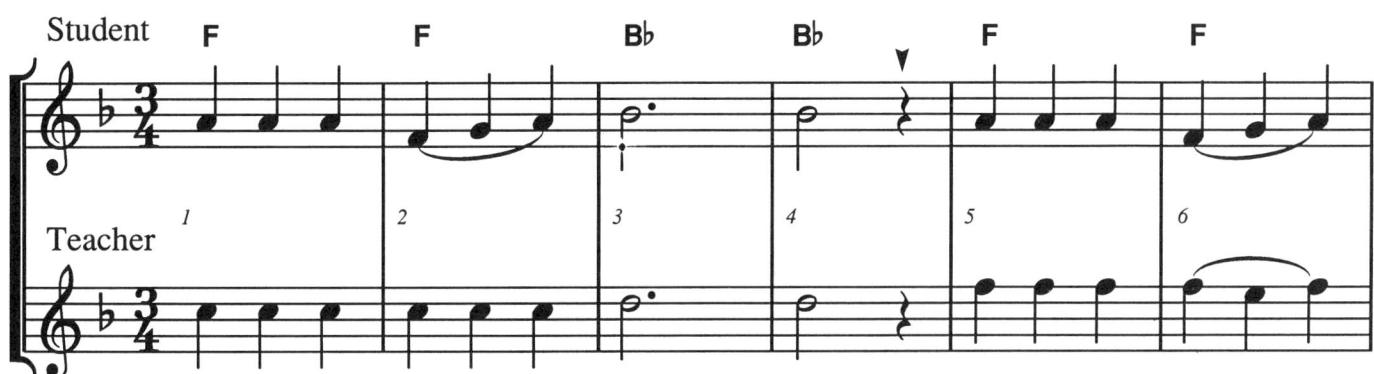

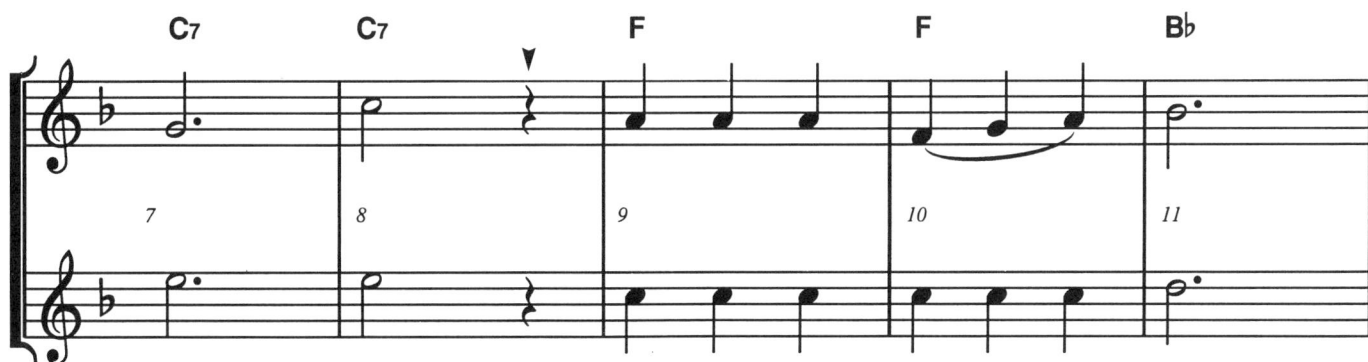

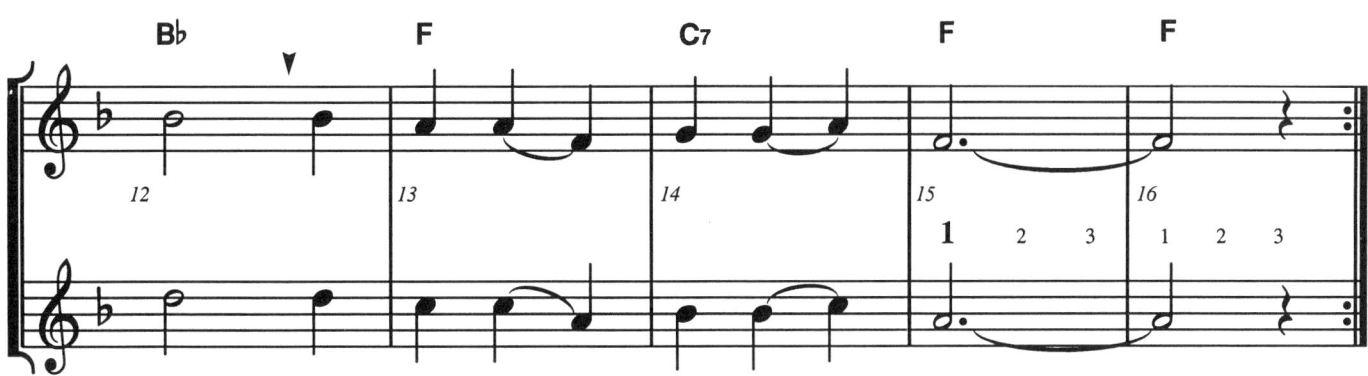

#  Roses from the South

Johann Strauss

Flat signs at the start of a line of music are called a **key signature**, which is explained on page 57. You do not need to know any new notes to play this song.

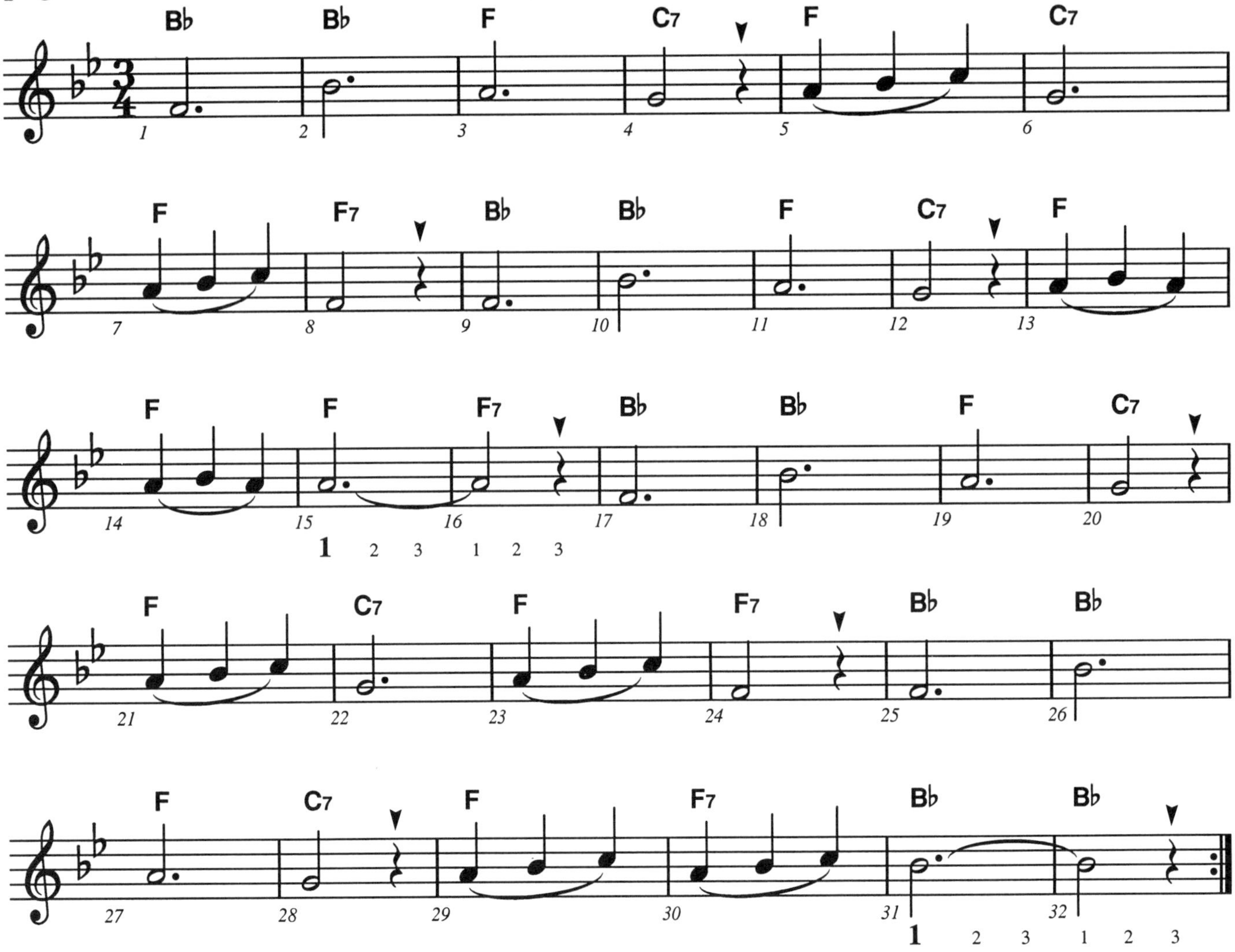

# The Whole Note

This is a **whole note** (or **semibreve**).
It lasts for **four** beats.
There is one whole note in one bar of $\frac{4}{4}$ time.

#  Good Evening Friends

# Lesson 7
## The Lead-in (or Pick-up)

Sometimes a song does not begin on the first beat of a bar. Any notes which come before the first full bar are called **lead-in notes** (or **pick-up notes**). When lead-in notes are used the last bar is also incomplete. The notes in the lead-in and the notes in the last bar add up to one full bar.

## The Banks of the Ohio

Traditional

On the cassette there are **five** drumbeats to introduce this song.

## The Mexican Hat Dance

Traditional Mexican

On the cassette there are **five** drumbeats to introduce this song.

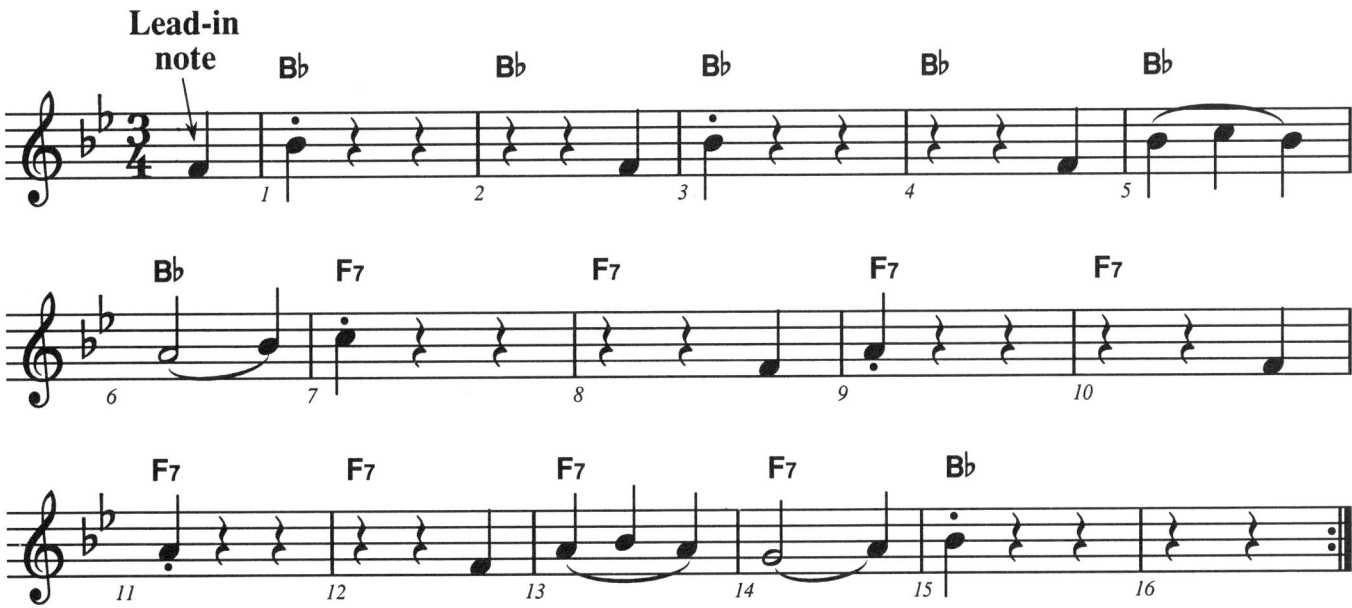

# When the Saints Go Marchin' In

Traditional

On the cassette there are **five** drumbeats to introduce this song.

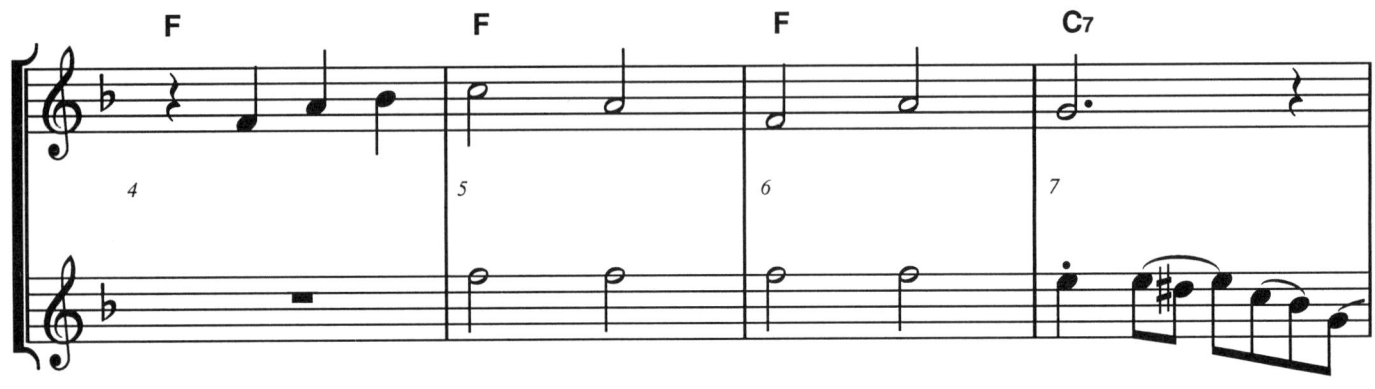

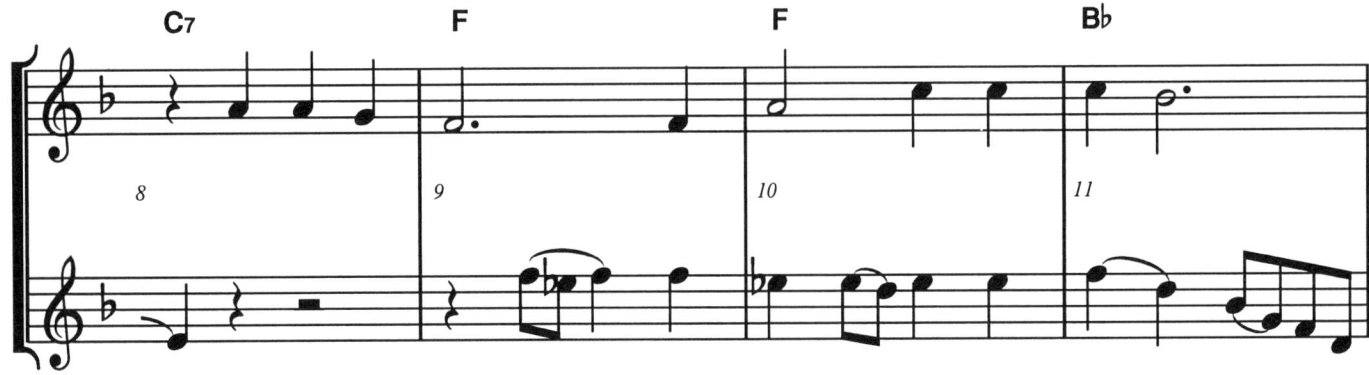

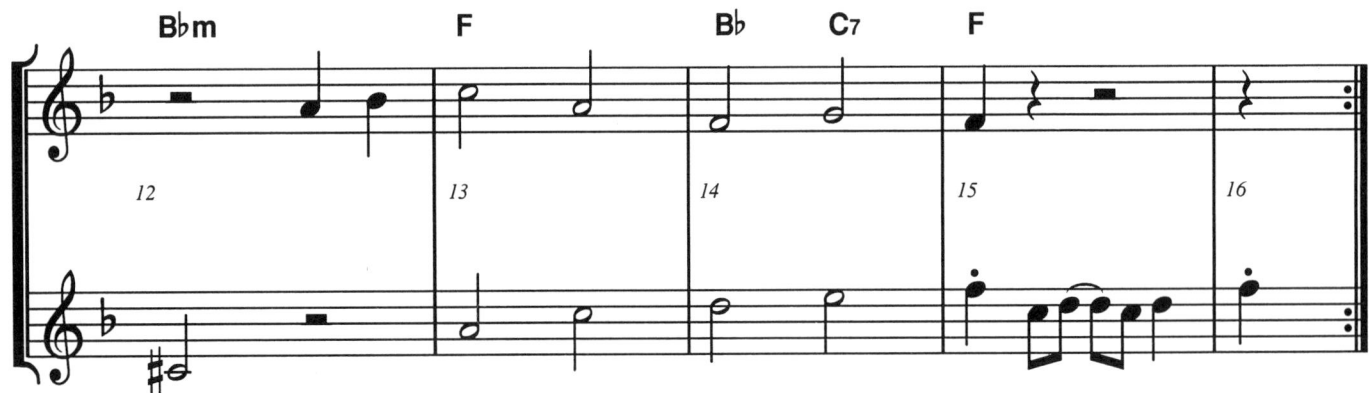

# Lesson 8
## The Effortless Breathing Technique

It is best if you have a teacher to help you understand this section.

### Step 1

Lie on your back on the floor, legs straight out. Place the palm of one hand over your navel. Make as if you are blowing your nose. Feel your muscles tighten underneath your hand as you do this. Continue blowing until the muscles are quite tight. Hold them tight for a few seconds. By this time you really need a breath. Let go those muscles you were blowing out with. Notice that your hand moves up and you get bigger round the waist as your new breath fills your lungs. Just relax your abdominal muscles and you will breathe in automatically.

### Step 2

Repeat Step 1. Observe that blowing out equals gentle effort, and breathing in equals relaxation. Now blow out through your mouth, very gently and slowly. Shape your lips as if you are playing the flute. Breathe in and out, over and over, until you think you understand.

### Step 3

Stand up and go through the cycle again. Don't try to suck air in. Think of an inflatable life-raft - you pull out the plug and floop!, it fills up by itself.

### Step 4

Play the exercises on the flute. Take breaths at the places marked, even if you don't need to.

**Remember:**    Breathe in  -  Relax
                         Blow out   -  Tighten gently.

## Exercise 15

Count slowly    relax        relax

## Exercise 16

## Exercise 17

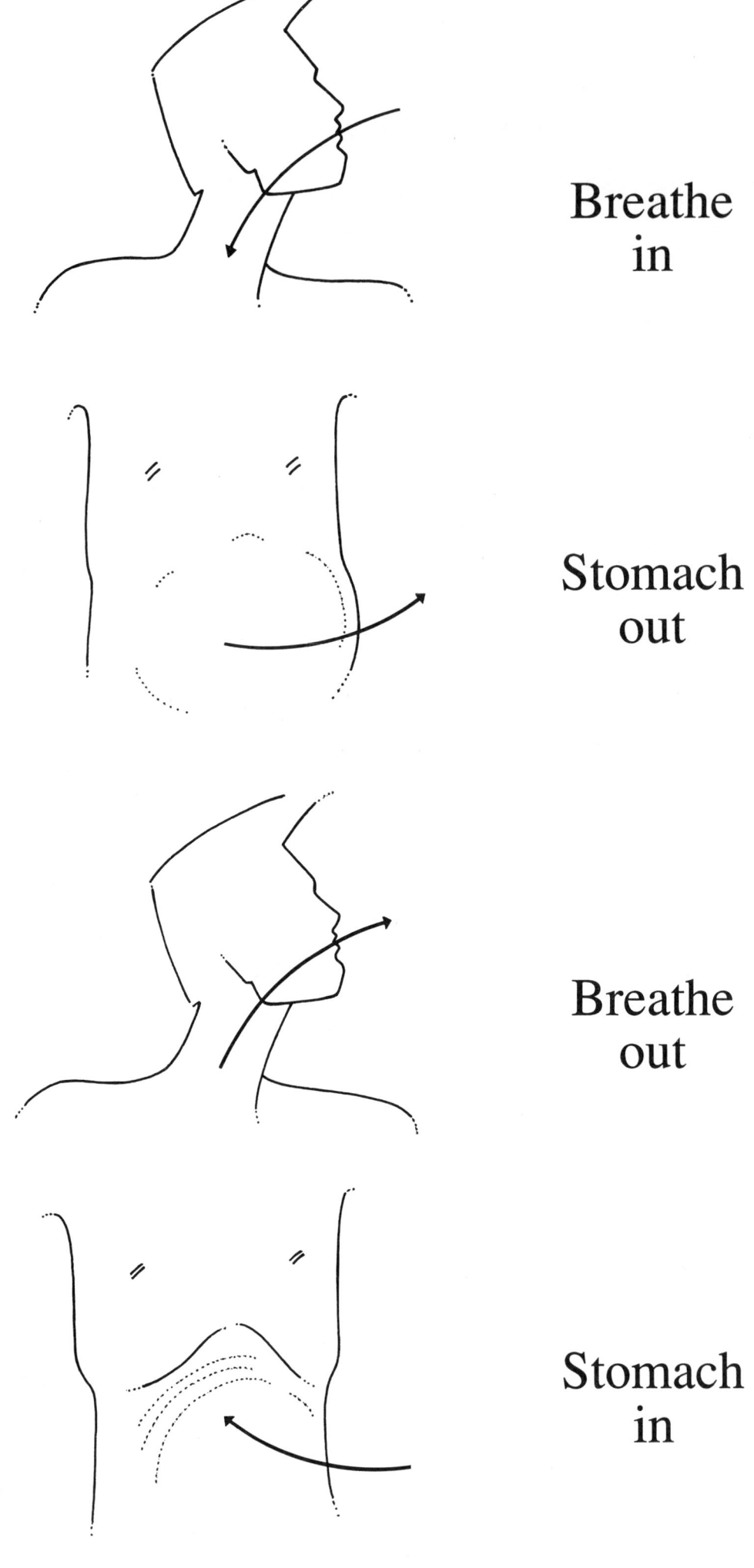

Breathe
in

Stomach
out

Breathe
out

Stomach
in

## Exercise 18

## Exercise 19

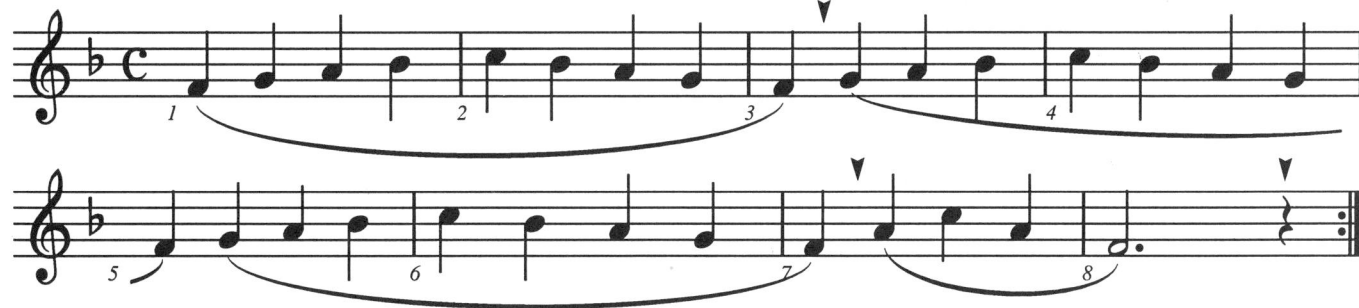

## Exercise 20

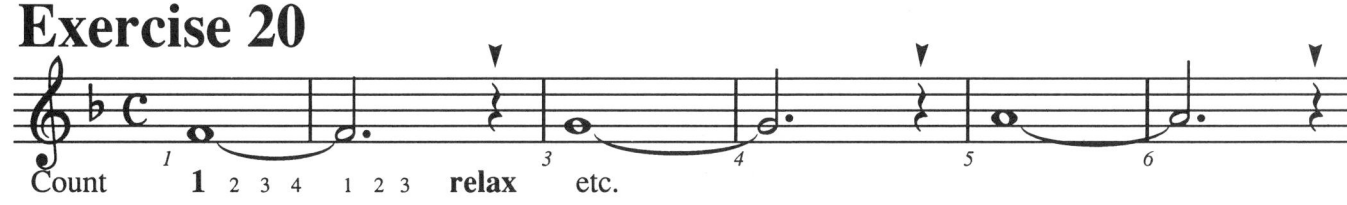

Count    **1**   2   3   4    1   2   3   **relax**    etc.

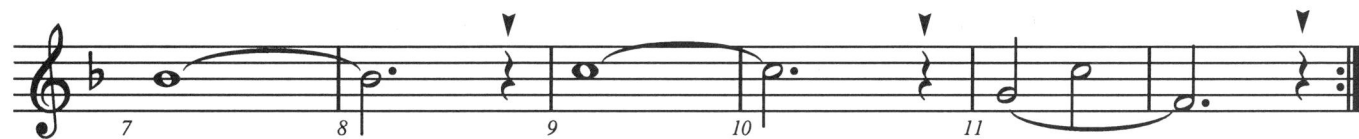

# Helpful Hints

1.  The more you can relax, the deeper your in-breath will be.
2.  When you blow out, think of a tube of toothpaste. If you squeeze it from the bottom, you use all the tooth-paste. But, if you squeeze from the top, some remains in the bottom. So it is with your lungs. Gently squeeze from your abdominal area and all the air will be used and you will have more control.
3.  This is yoga breathing.
4.  When you use this method, you fill up your lungs from the very bottom. The breaths will be deeper and quicker than before.
5.  The process may seem contrary to everything you have learnt in life about breathing. If it is, good. You will be more healthy as a result of learning this. When you have mastered it, you will see how natural it is. You will find yourself breathing this way 24 hours a day.
6.  You may not see much movement of your belly at first when you breathe in. When you can relax those muscles more fully, there will be more motion visible.
7.  Practice the technique at other times, walking, waiting for the bus, driving. No-one will be able to tell.

**Remember this above all else:**
**Breathe in**     =     **Relax**
**Blow out**     =     **Gentle effort**

When you are doing it right, it gets easier and easier.

# Lesson 9
## The Note E

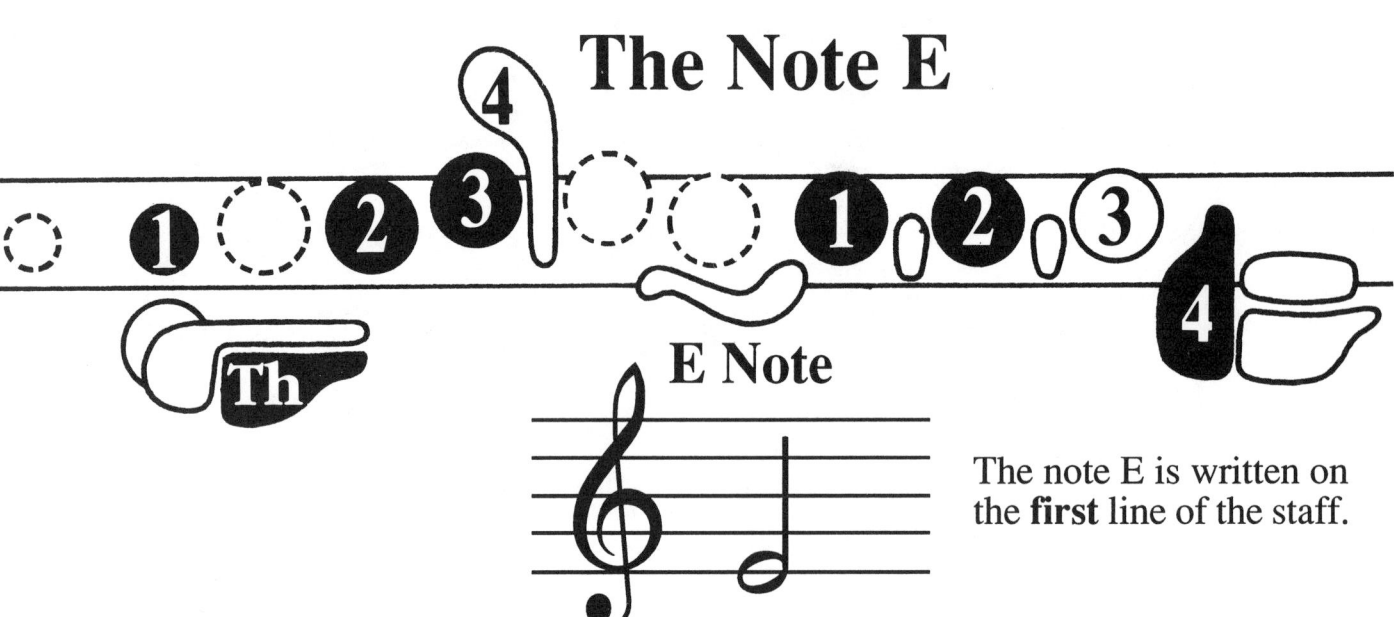

**E Note**

The note E is written on the **first** line of the staff.

When you play the lower notes on the flute, you will need to adjust your embouchure (mouth position). You will find that the lower notes are softer and have more breath in them. For low notes, try blowing the flute a little more, and allowing the mouthpiece to move downwards, so that your lips can obtain the best position.

## Exercise 21

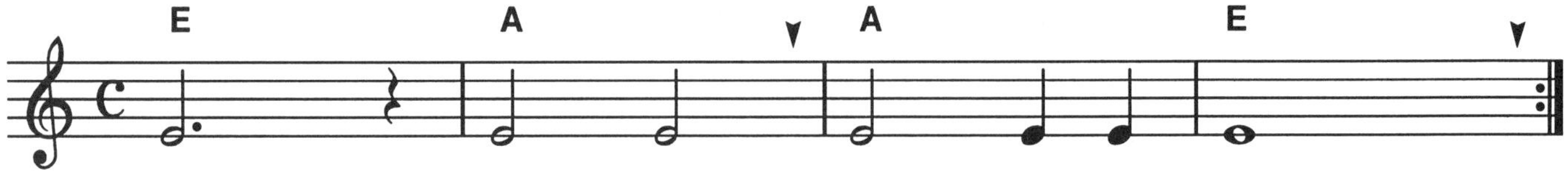

## Flute Waltz 1

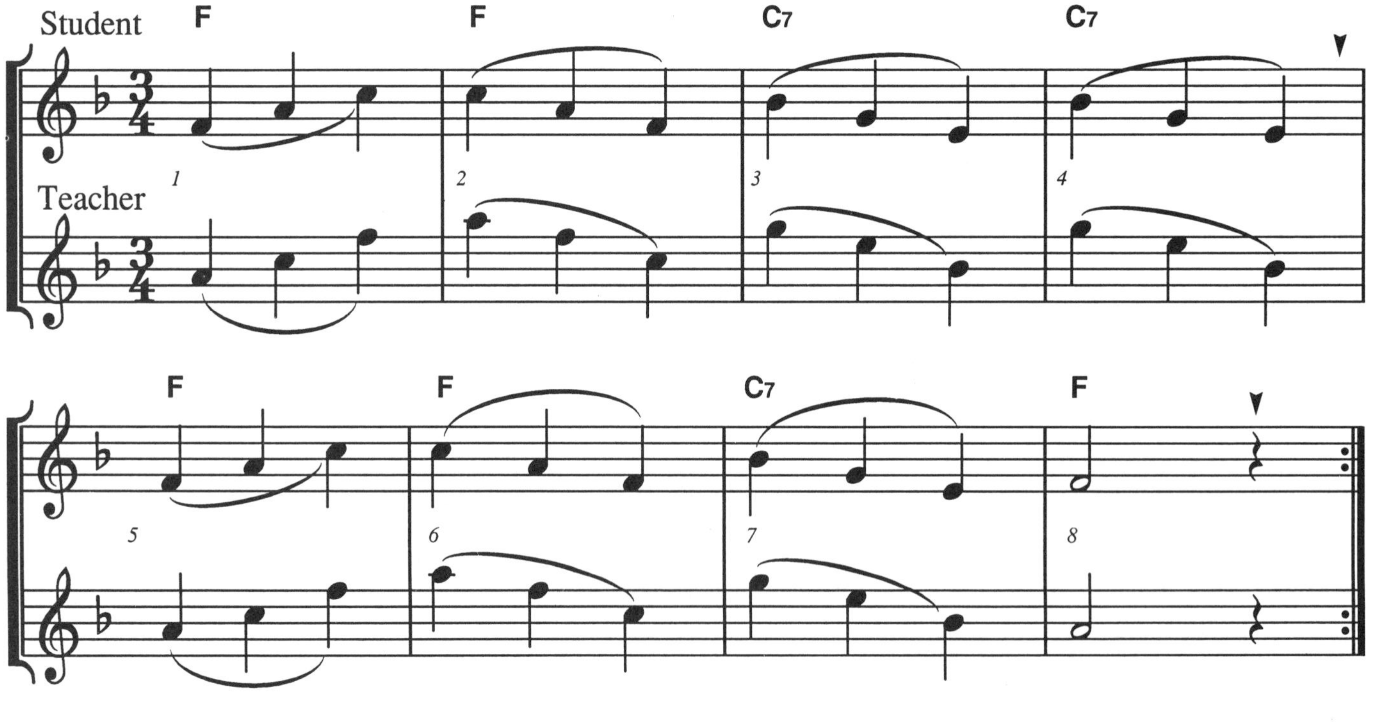

## 📼 Mary Ann

Traditional

# First and Second Endings

The next song contains **first and second endings**. The first time you play through the song, play the first ending then go back to the beginning. The second time you play through the song, play the second ending instead of the first.

In Flute Waltz 2 play through to the end of the first ending (bar 8), then repeat the song from the beginning as indicated by the repeat dots. When you play through the song the second time, do not play bars 7 and 8 again (the first ending), but play bars 9 and 10 (the second ending).

## 📼 Flute Waltz 2

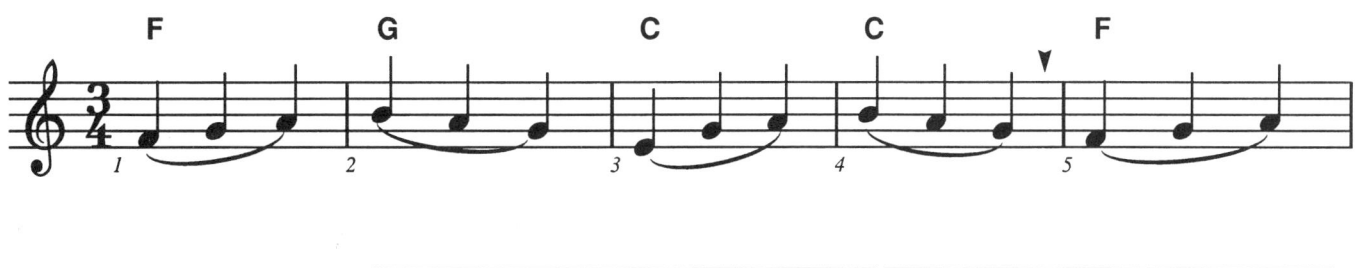

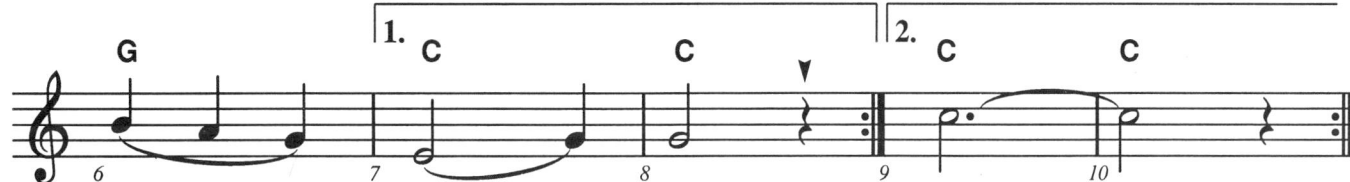

# Melody in F

Ludwig van Beethoven

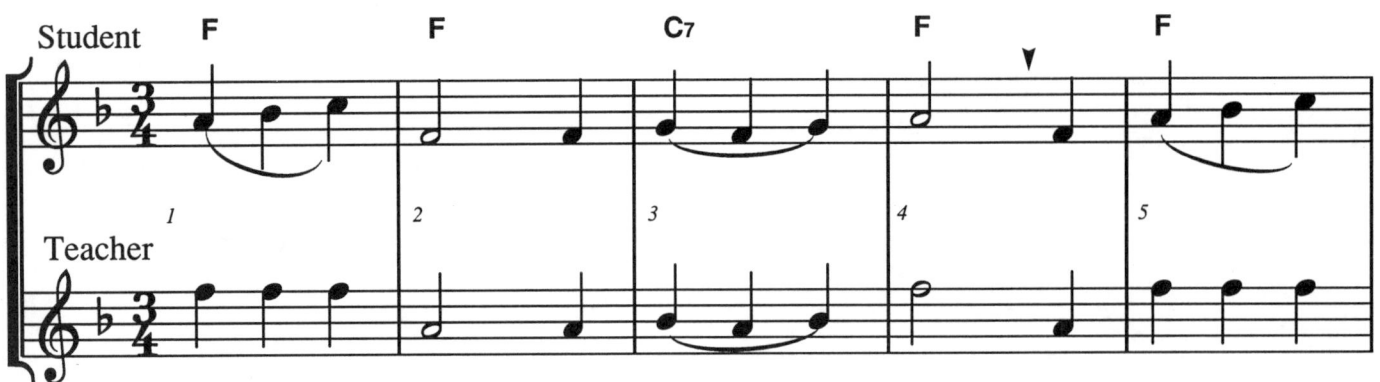

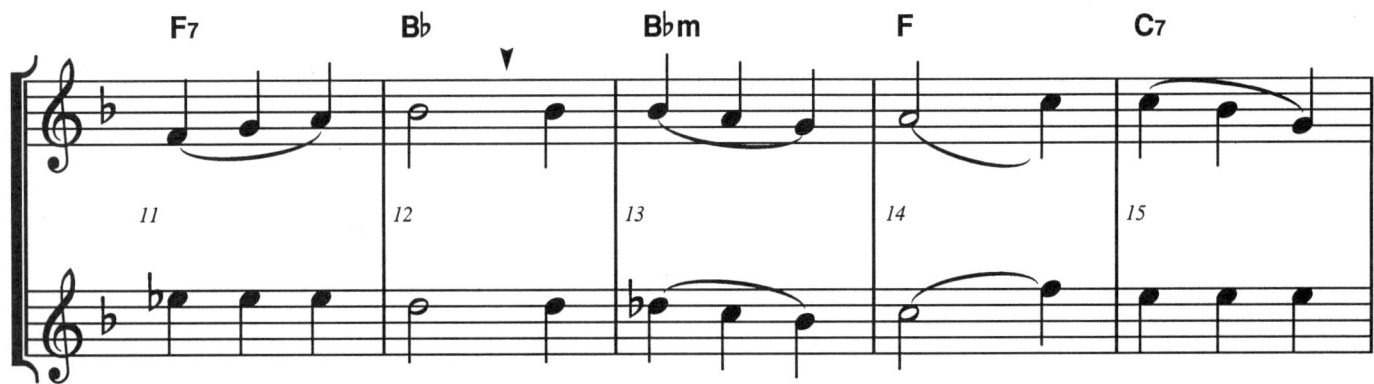

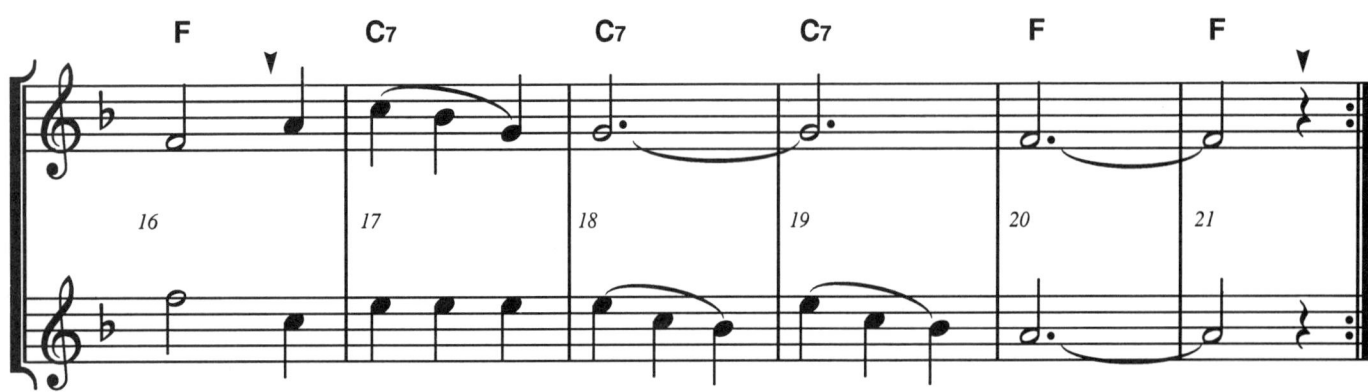

# Lesson 10

## The Eighth Note

This is an **eighth** note (or **quaver**). There are eight eighth notes in one bar of 4/4 time. When eighth notes are joined together, the tails are replaced by one **beam**.

**Tail**

**Beam**

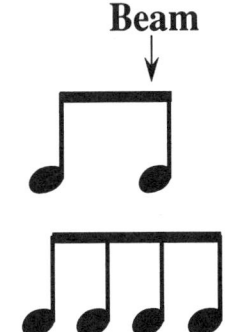

Two eighth notes joined together.

Four eighth notes joined together.

# How to Count Eighth Notes

## Exercise 22

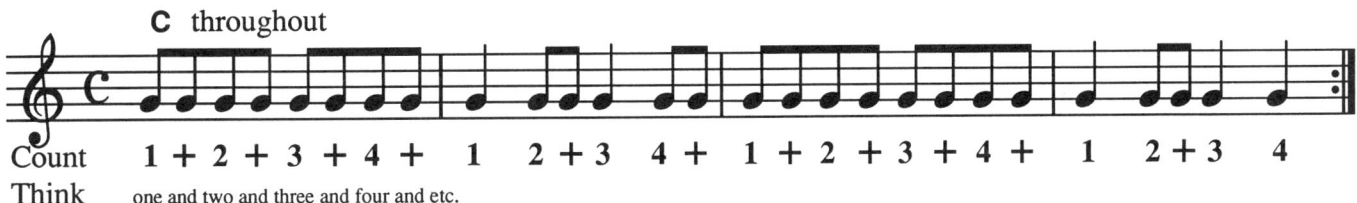

Count    1 + 2 + 3 + 4 +    1   2 + 3   4 +    1 + 2 + 3 + 4 +    1   2 + 3   4

Think    one and two and three and four and etc.

## Shave and a Haircut

Traditional

Count    1    2 + 3    4        1    2    3

## Rock Riff 1

## Mick's Mexican Mix

Traditional

On the cassette there are **five** drumbeats to introduce this song.

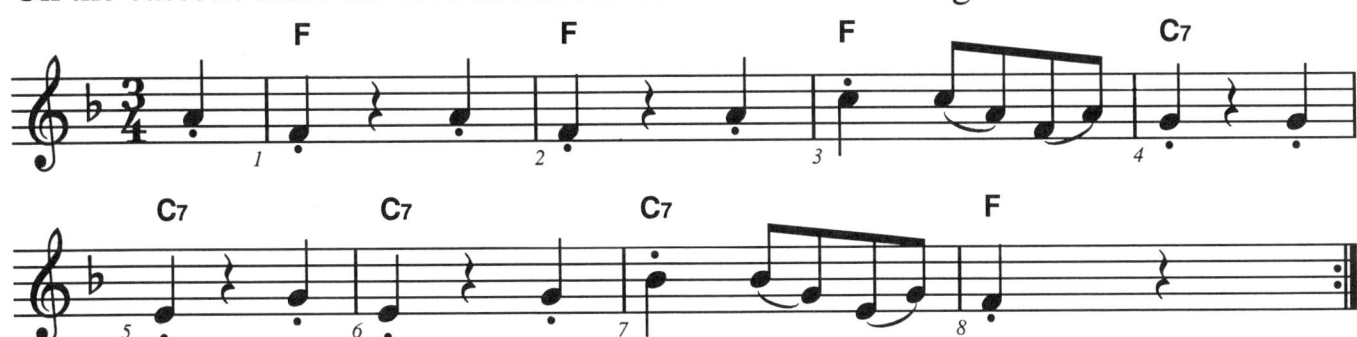

# The Note D

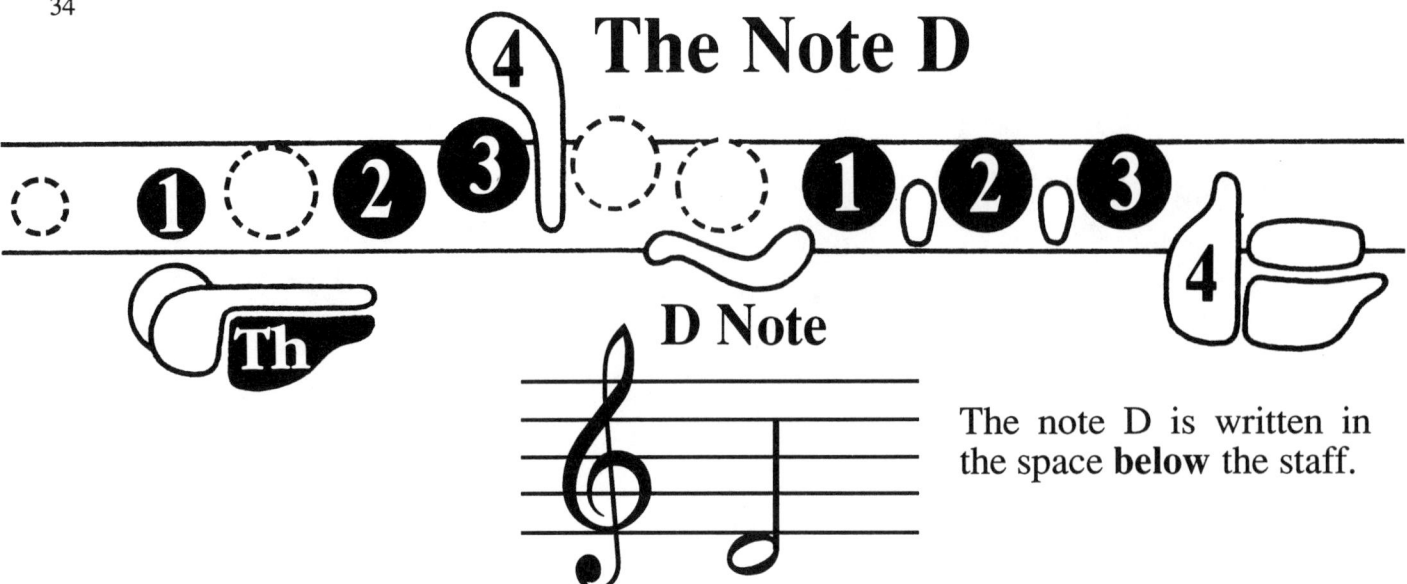

## D Note

The note D is written in the space **below** the staff.

Each note sounds at its best when your lips are in a very precise place. It may be difficult to make this note sound as crisp as A and G. Experiment with your lips to find the best position and shape for them to produce D.

## 📼 Exercise 23

## 📼 Big Ben

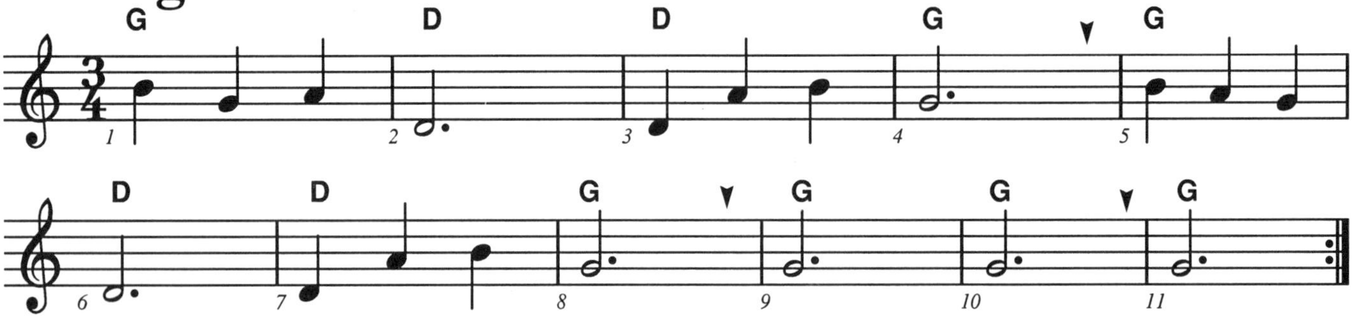

## 📼 Harem Dance

Traditional

On the cassette there are **six** drumbeats to introduce this song.

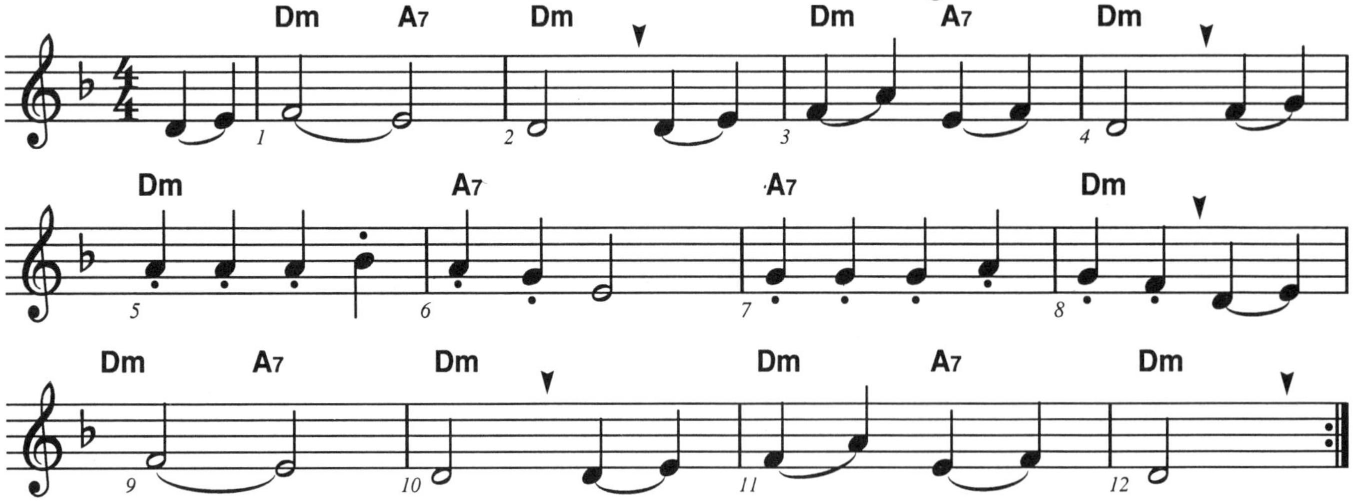

# The Volga Boatman

Traditional Russian

# La Spagnola

Traditional

# Lesson 11
## The Note D in the Middle Register

### The Registers of the Flute

A **register** on an instrument is a range of notes that have similar qualities of tone. On the flute there are three registers. All the notes you have learnt so far have been in the low register.

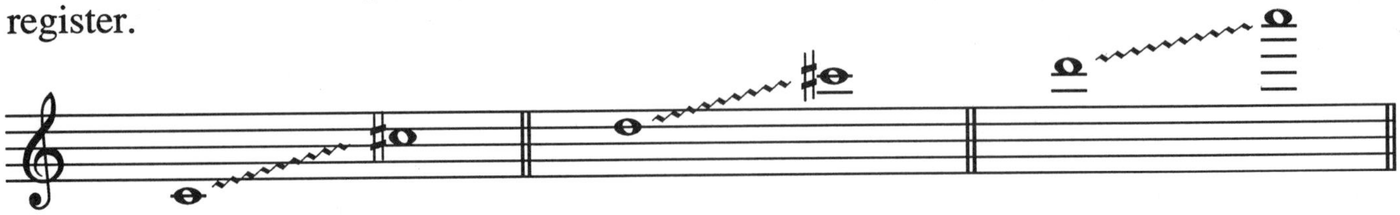

**Low Register**
Warm, mellow, dark

**Middle Register**
Sweet, fluid, light

**High Register**
Bright, dramatic, piercing

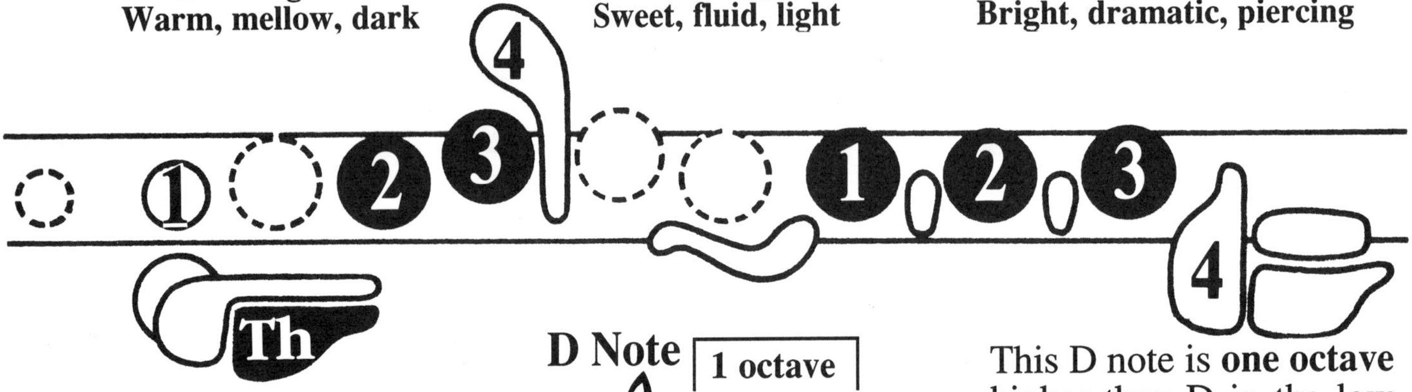

**D Note** | 1 octave |

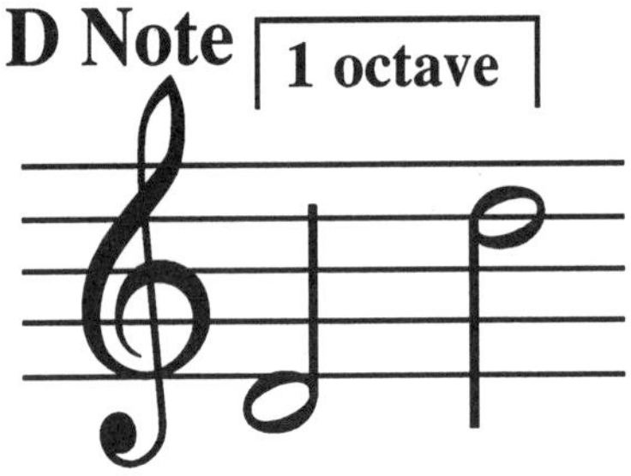

This D note is **one octave** higher than D in the low register. An octave is the distance between one note and another note above (or below) it with the same letter name.

### 📼 Exercise 24

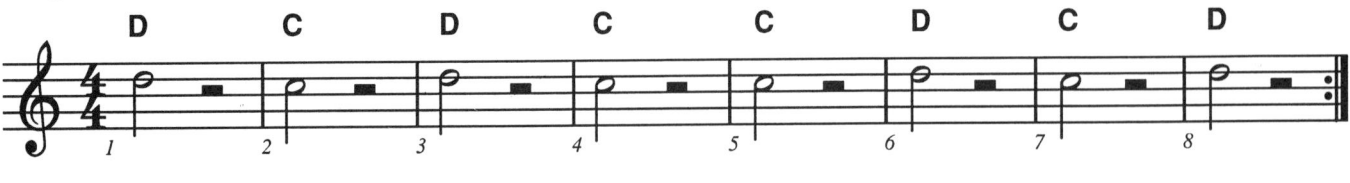

| Dm | | D | | D | Dm | | D |

### 📼 Exercise 25

Now you come to the hard part. You have to change from D to C and back again without dropping the flute. This involves moving from seven fingers on the flute for D, to three fingers on the flute for C.

| D | C | D | C | C | D | C | D |
| 1 | 2 | 3 | 4 | 5 | 6 | 7 | 8 |

### 📼 Exercise 26

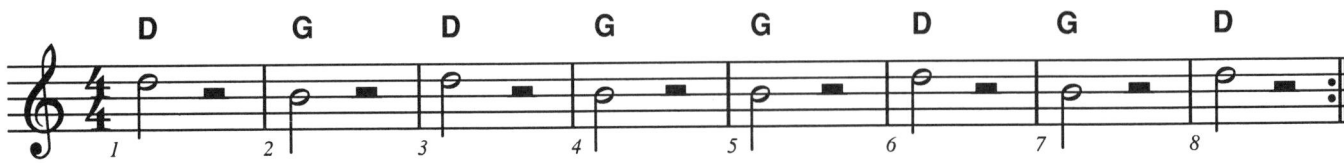

| D | G | D | G | G | D | G | D |
| 1 | 2 | 3 | 4 | 5 | 6 | 7 | 8 |

 # Exercise 27

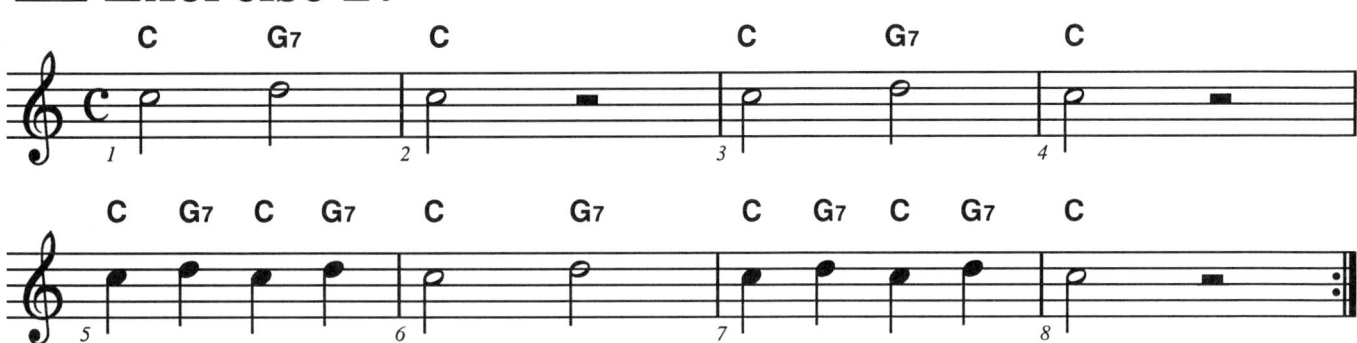

# 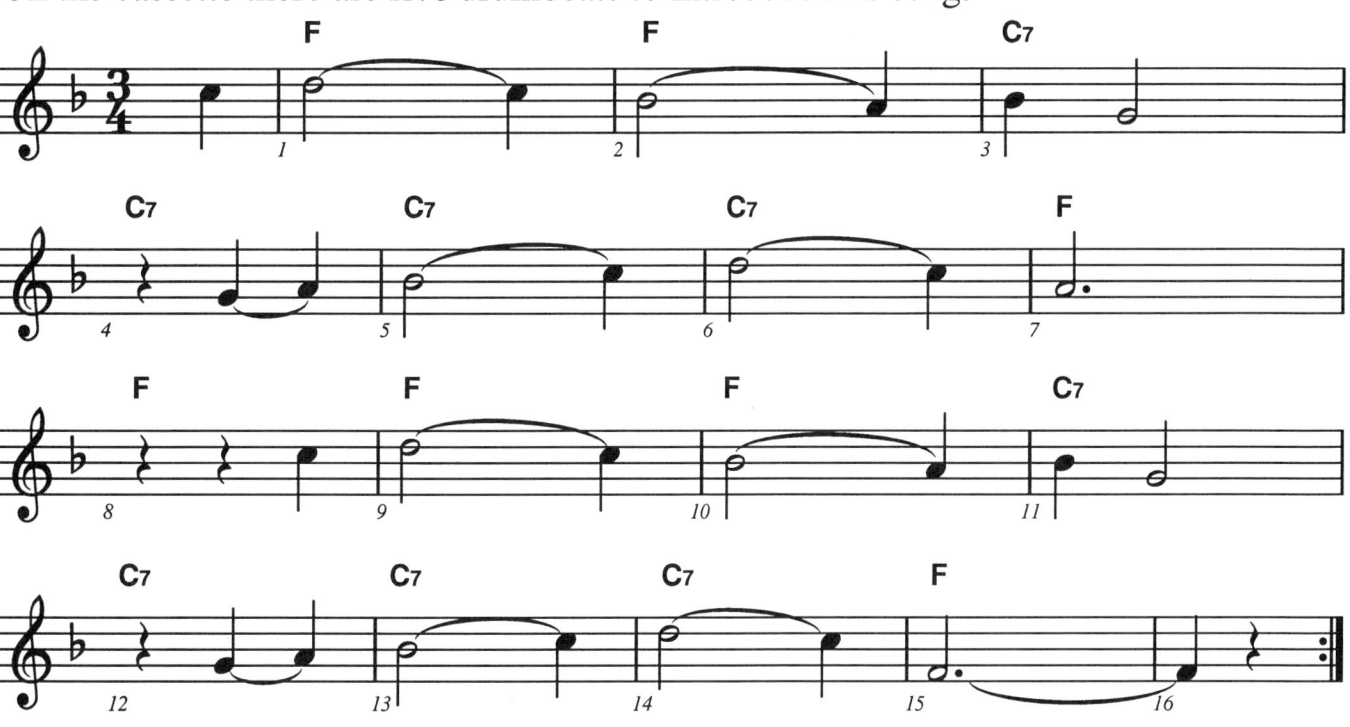The Carnival of Venice

Traditional

On the cassette there are **five** drumbeats to introduce this song.

# Goodnight Irene

Traditional

# 🔊 Blow the Man Down

Traditional

On the cassette there are **five** drumbeats to introduce this song.

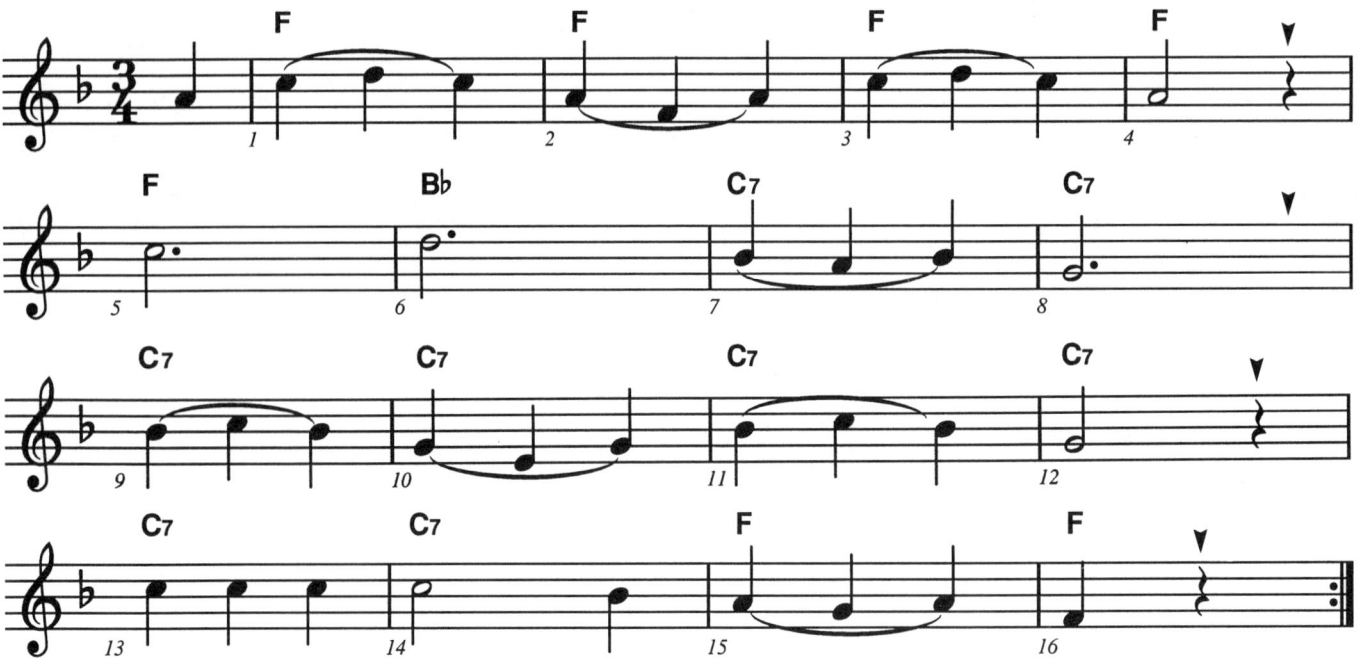

# 🔊 When Johnny Comes Marching Home

Traditional

On the cassette there are **five** drumbeats to introduce this song.

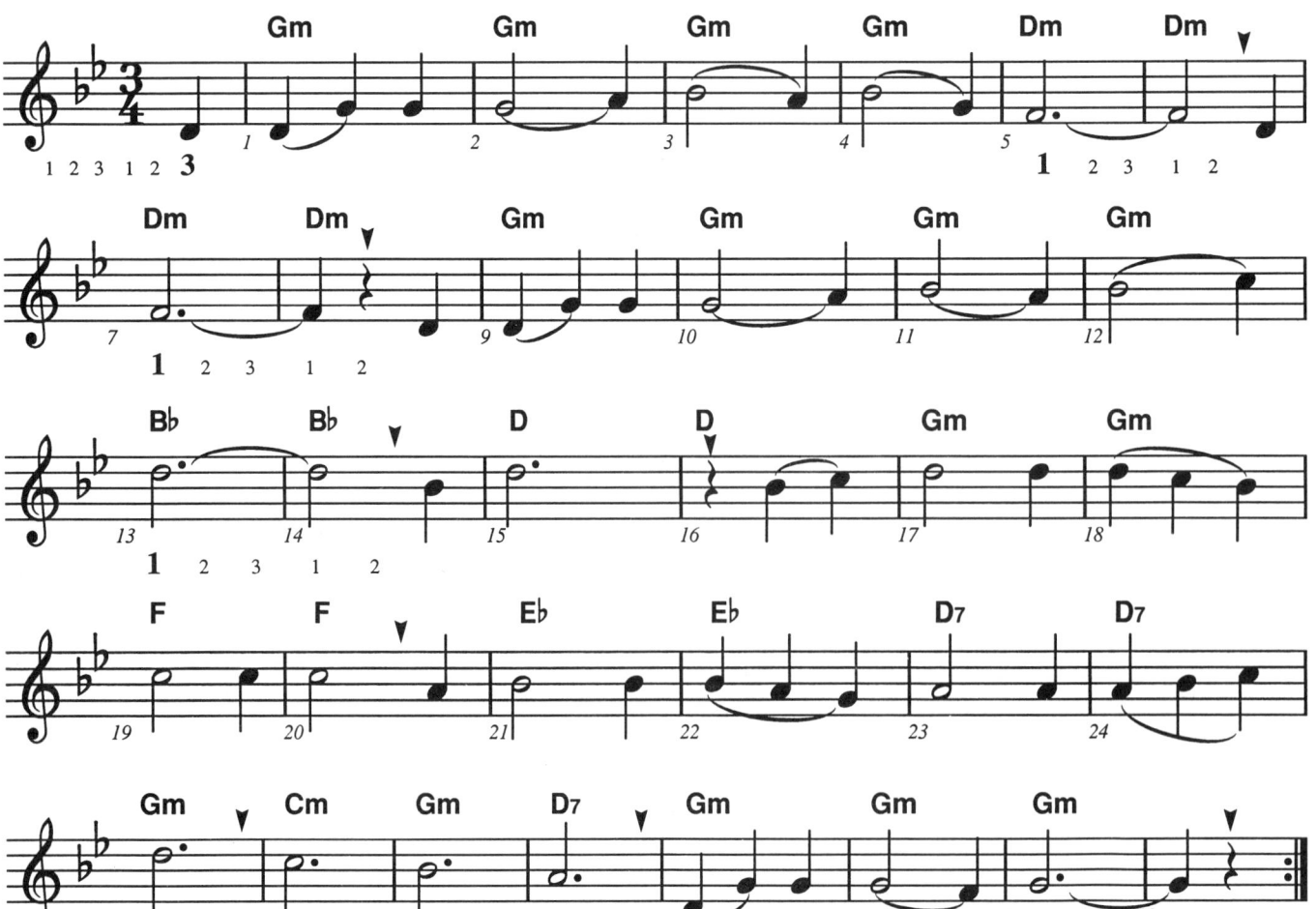

##  There's a Hole in the Bucket

Traditional

On the cassette there are **five** drumbeats to introduce this song.

## For He's a Jolly Good Fellow

Traditional

On the cassette there are **five** drumbeats to introduce this song.

***D.C. al Fine*** (pronounced "fee-nay")

Over bar 24 the instruction ***D.C. Al Fine*** is written. This means that you play the song again from the beginning until you reach the word ***Fine***.

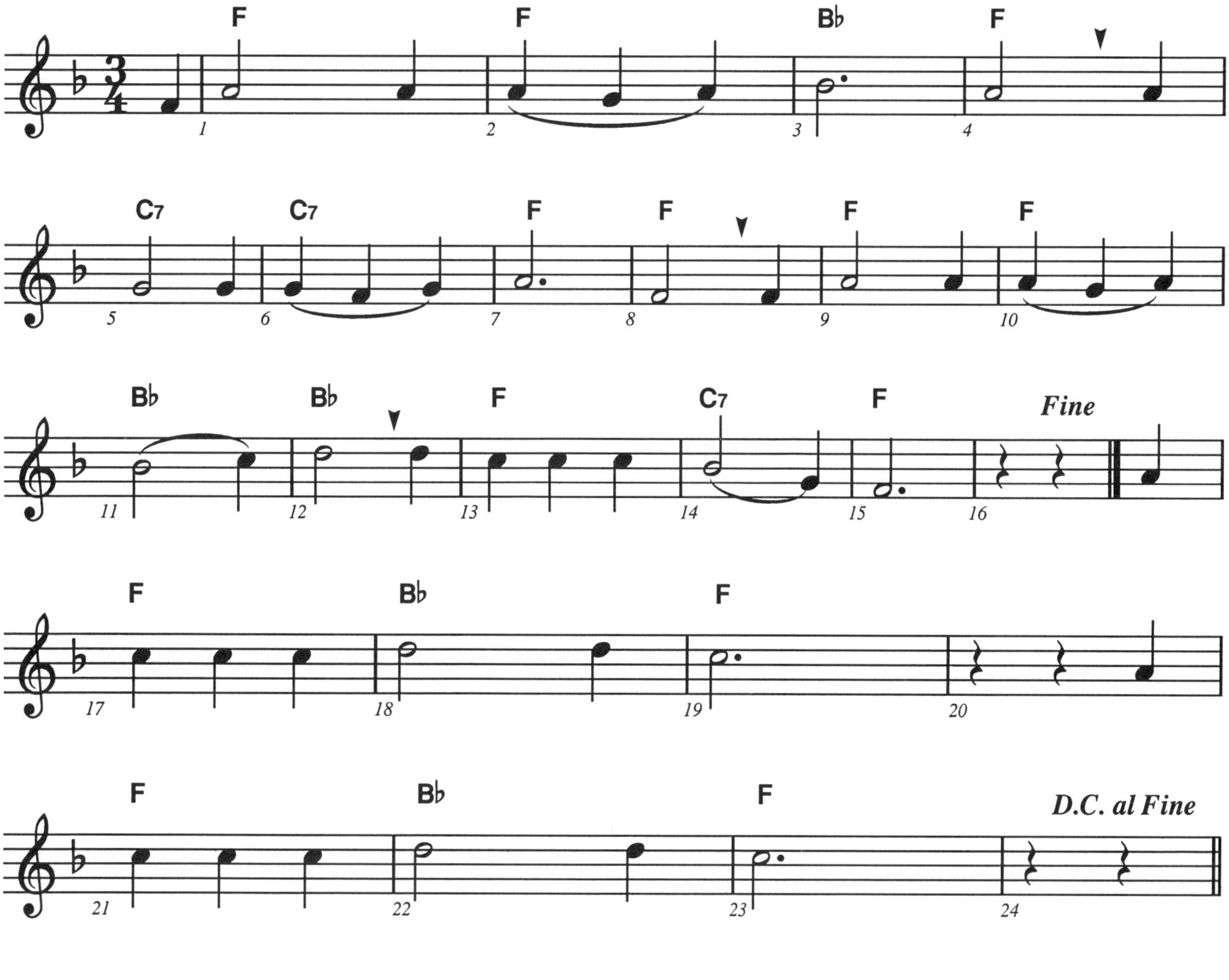

# Lesson 12
## The Dotted Quarter Note

A dot written after a quarter note means that you hold the note for **one and a half beats**. A dotted quarter note is often followed by an eighth note.

### 🎴 Exercise 28

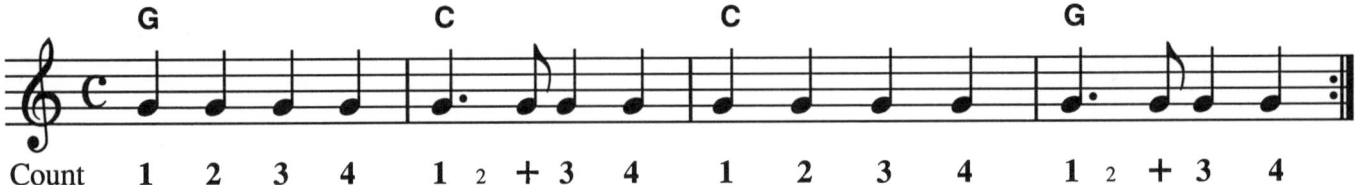

Count   **1**   **2**   **3**   **4**    **1**   2   **+**   **3**   **4**    **1**   **2**   **3**   **4**    **1**   2   **+**   **3**   **4**

### 🎴 Home Sweet Home

Traditional

On the cassette there are **three** drumbeats to introduce this song.

Count 1 2 3 **4 +**

### 🎴 Jingle Bells

Traditional

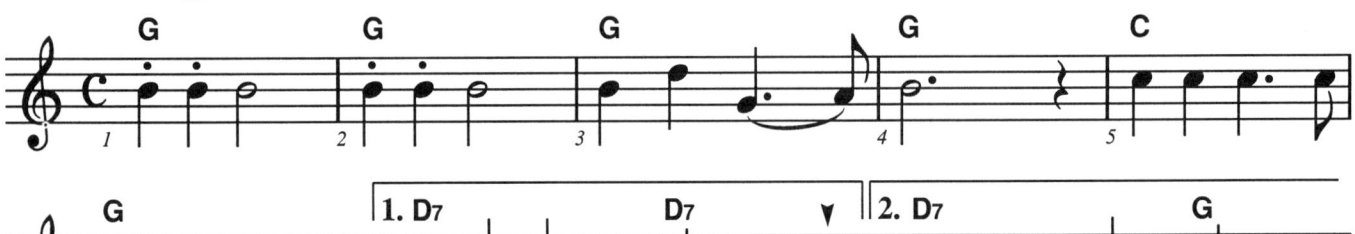

### 🎴 Cockles and Mussels

James Yorston

On the cassette there are **five** drumbeats to introduce this song.

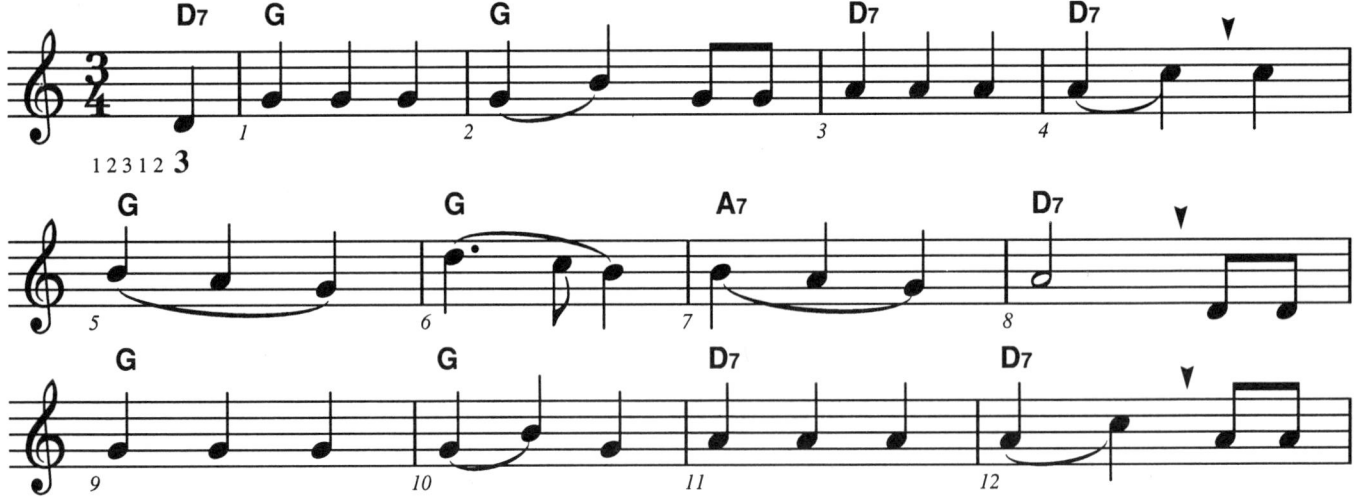

## O Susanna

Stephen Foster

On the cassette there are **three** drumbeats to introduce this song.

# Lesson 13
## Sharp Signs

 This is a **sharp** sign.

### The Note F Sharp (F♯)

A sharp sign raises the pitch of the note to which it applies by an interval of one semitone. Thus the note F♯ is one semitone **higher** than F. Since the difference in pitch between the notes F and G is one whole tone (two semitones), F♯ is also one semitone **lower** than G.

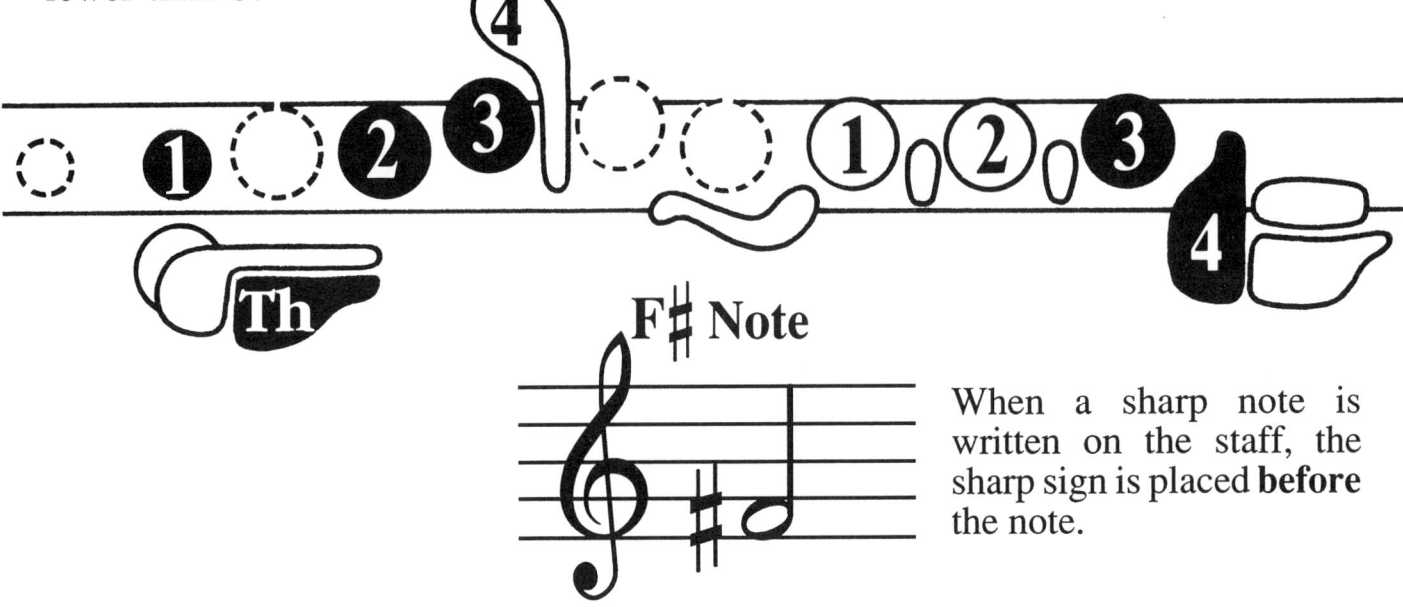

**F♯ Note**

When a sharp note is written on the staff, the sharp sign is placed **before** the note.

## 🔊 Exercise 29

## 🔊 The Galway Piper

Traditional

# 📼 The Daring Young Man on the Flying Trapeze

On the cassette there are **five** drumbeats to introduce this song.                    Traditional

Instead of writing a sharp sign before every F♯ note, it is easier to write just one sharp sign after the treble clef. This means that all F notes on the staff are played as F♯, even though there is no sharp sign placed before the note.

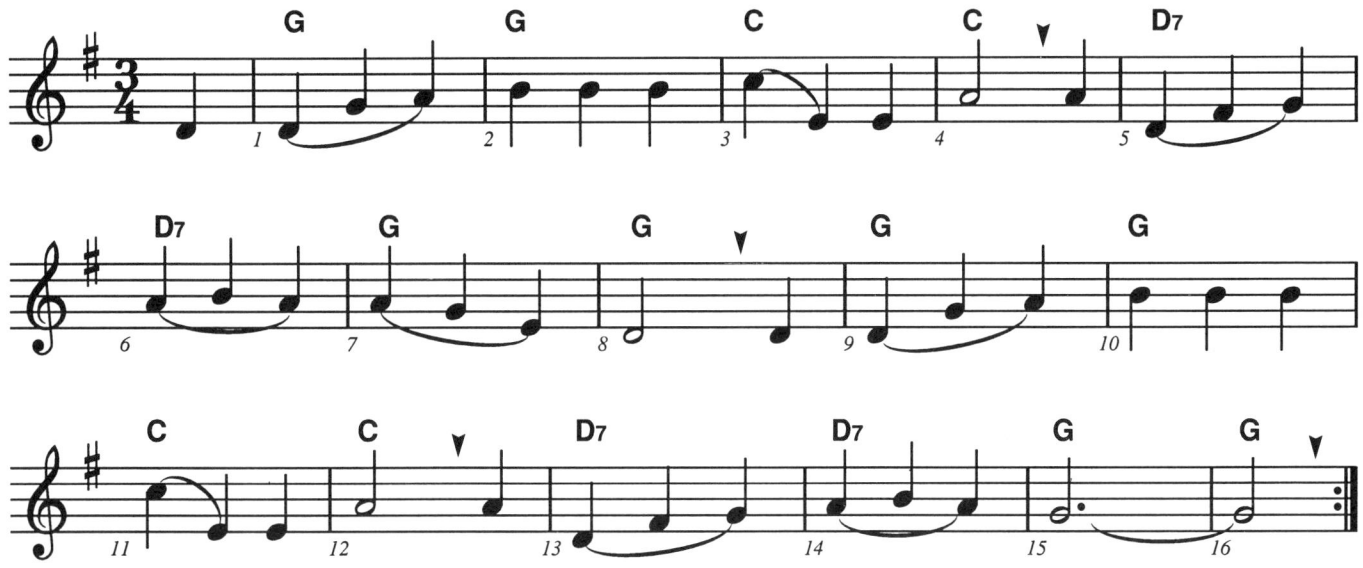

# 📼 We Wish You a Merry Christmas

Traditional

On the cassette there are **five** drumbeats to introduce this song.

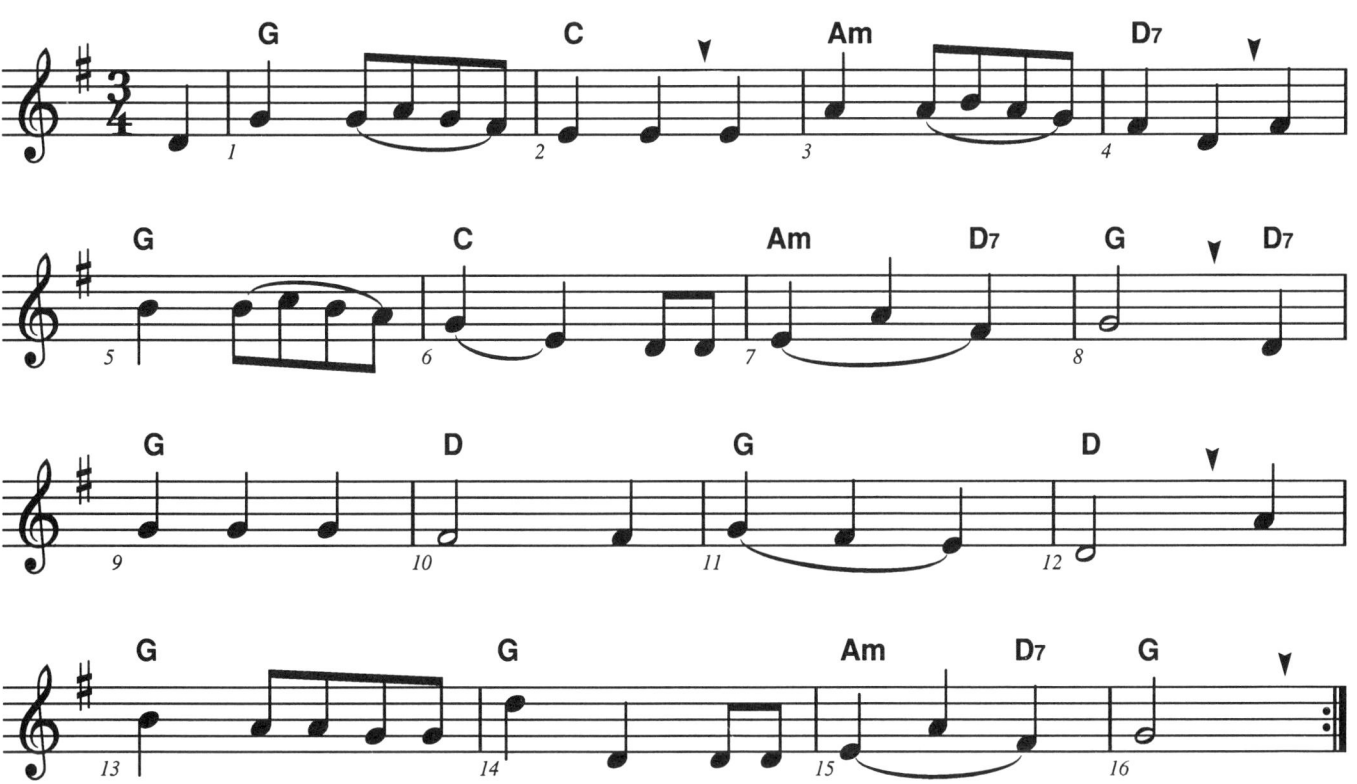

#  A Bicycle Built for Two

Traditional

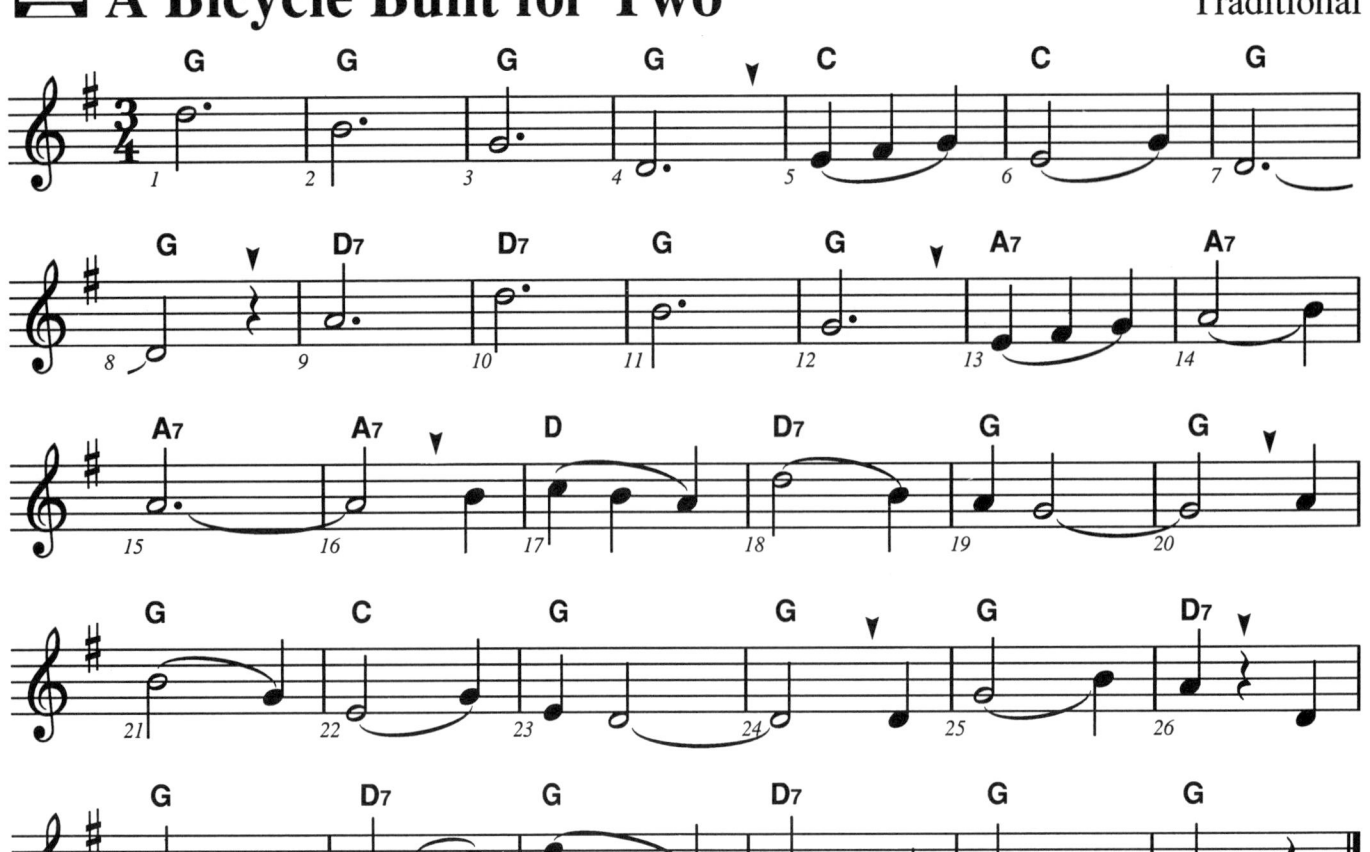

#  I-yi-yi-yi (Cielito Lindo)

Traditional

On the cassette there are **five** drumbeats to introduce this song.

# 📼 Aloha Oe

Traditional Hawaiian

On the cassette there are **three** drumbeats to introduce this song.

# 📼 Gypsy Song

Traditional

When a sharp or flat sign is written immediately before a note, it applies to the whole bar. E.g. in bar 3 of Gypsy Song, all the notes are played as F♯, even though only the first F note has a sharp sign in front of it. In bars 4 and 7 there are two F♯ notes in each bar.

# Lesson 14
## The Note E in the Middle Register

**E Note**

This E note is written in the **fourth** space of the staff. The fingering for this E is the same as for the E in the low register.

Middle E will sound more easily if you purse your lips slightly, as you do when you whistle. Try to avoid turning the flute inwards, because this action covers up more of the tone hole, making the sound muffled. Sometimes it helps to blow a little harder, but the most important factor is the position of your lips.

## Exercise 30

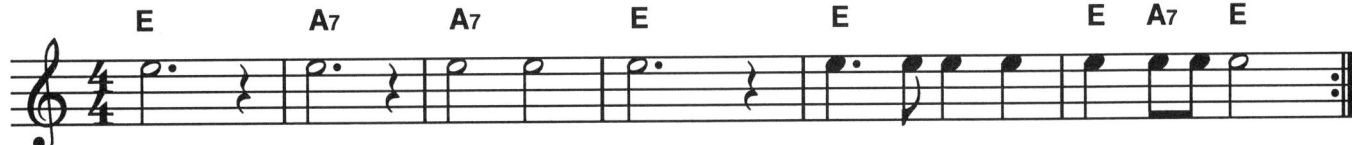

## Changing D to E

This is not as difficult as C to D, but it can be tricky co-ordinating the three fingers involved.

## Exercise 31

## Exercise 32

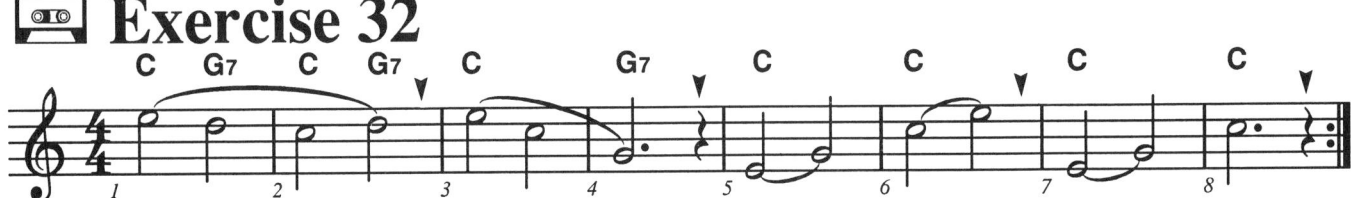

## Reveille

Traditional

On the cassette there are **three** drumbeats to introduce this song.

C throughout

## 🎛 Shortnin' Bread

Traditional

Sometimes a sharp sign is written at the start of a line even when there is no F note in the piece.

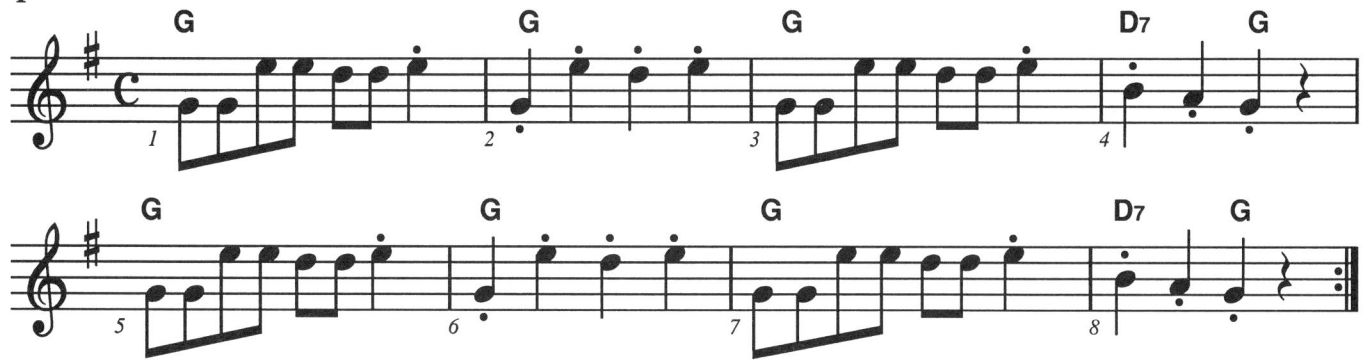

## 🎛 The Irish Washerwoman

Traditional

This song is a duet for two students.
On the cassette there are **four** drumbeats to introduce this song.

# My Bonnie Lies Over the Ocean

Traditional

On the cassette there are **five** drumbeats to introduce this song.

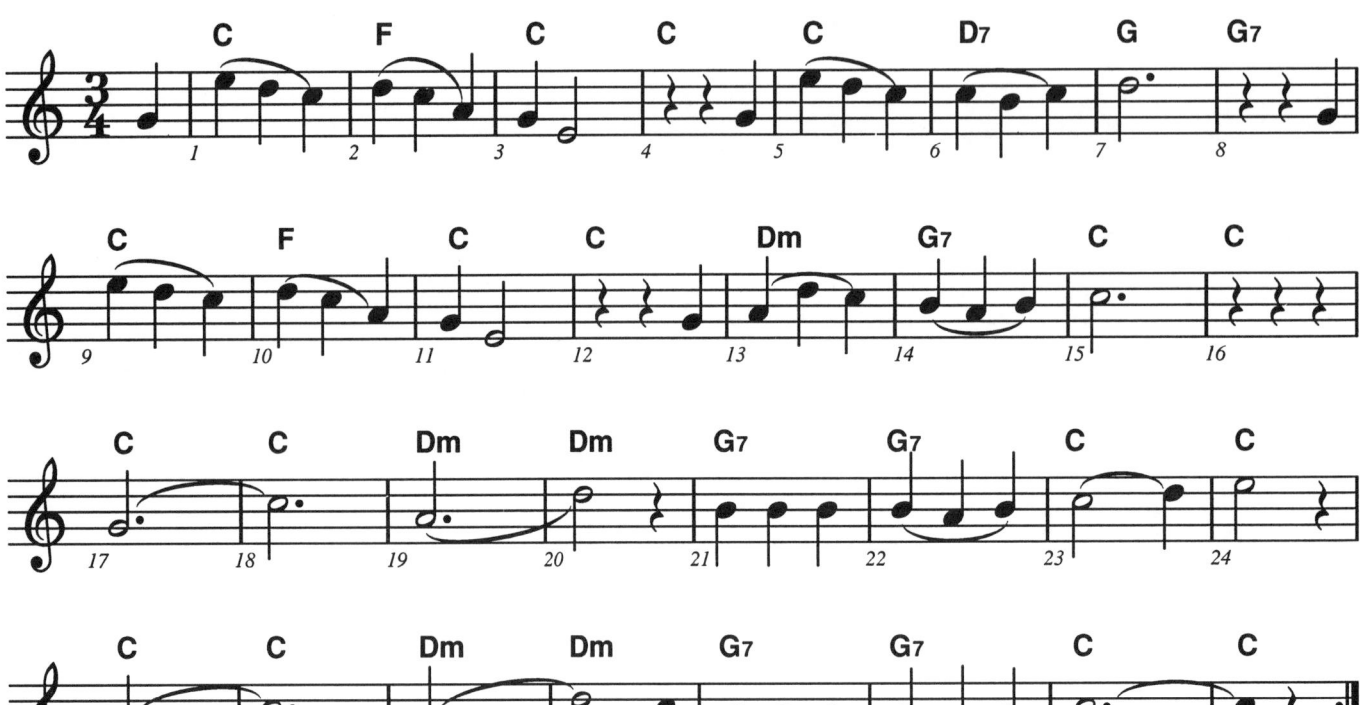

# The Eighth Rest

This is an **eighth rest** (or **quaver** rest).
Its value is **half** a beat.

# Exercise 33

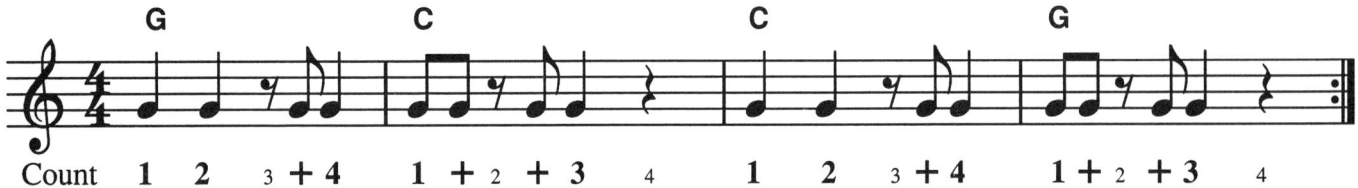

Count  1  2  3 + 4  1 + 2 + 3  4  1  2  3 + 4  1 + 2 + 3  4

# The 1812 Overture

Peter Tschaikowsky

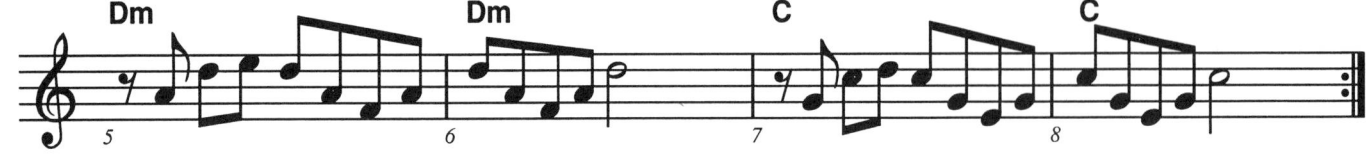

# Lesson 15
## The Note F in the Middle Register

The fingering for this F is the same as for the F you already know. Have your lips in the same position as you did for E.

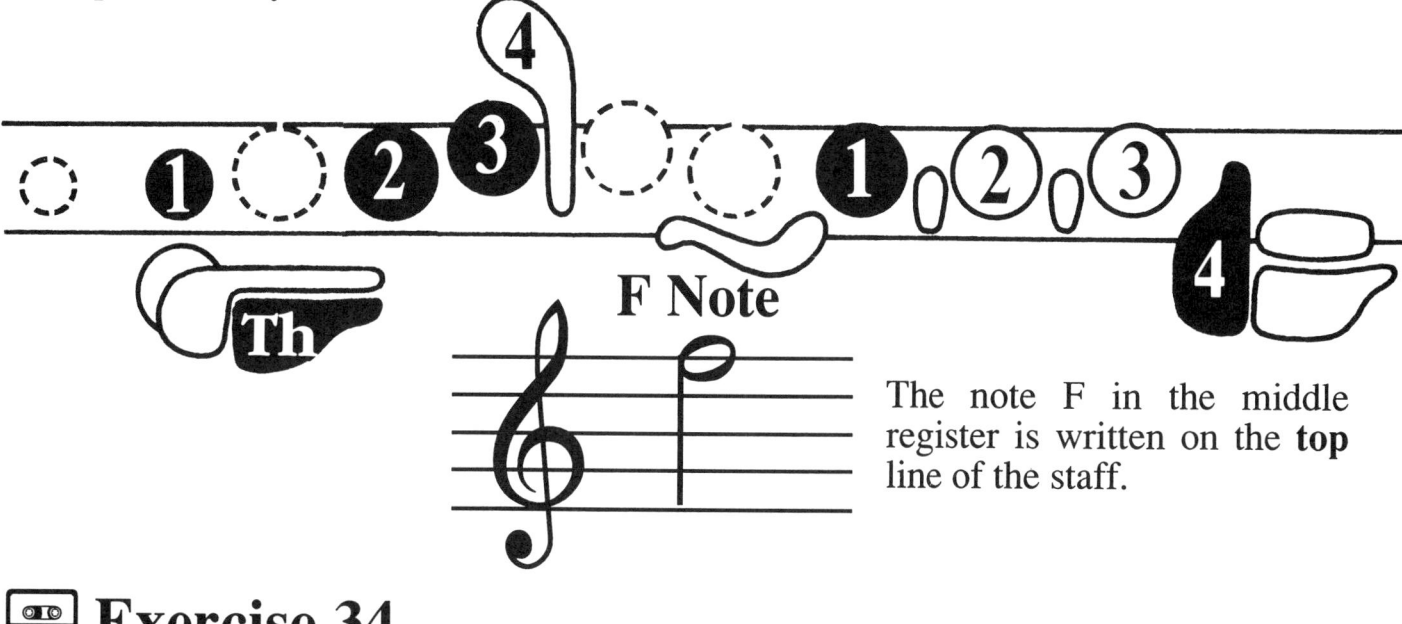

The note F in the middle register is written on the **top** line of the staff.

## 🔲 Exercise 34

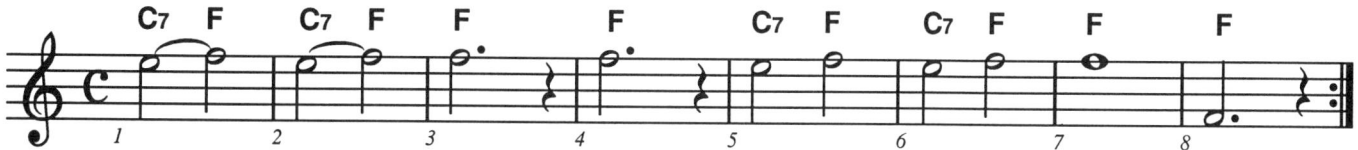

## 🔲 Exercise 35

## 🔲 Pick a Bale o' Cotton

Traditional

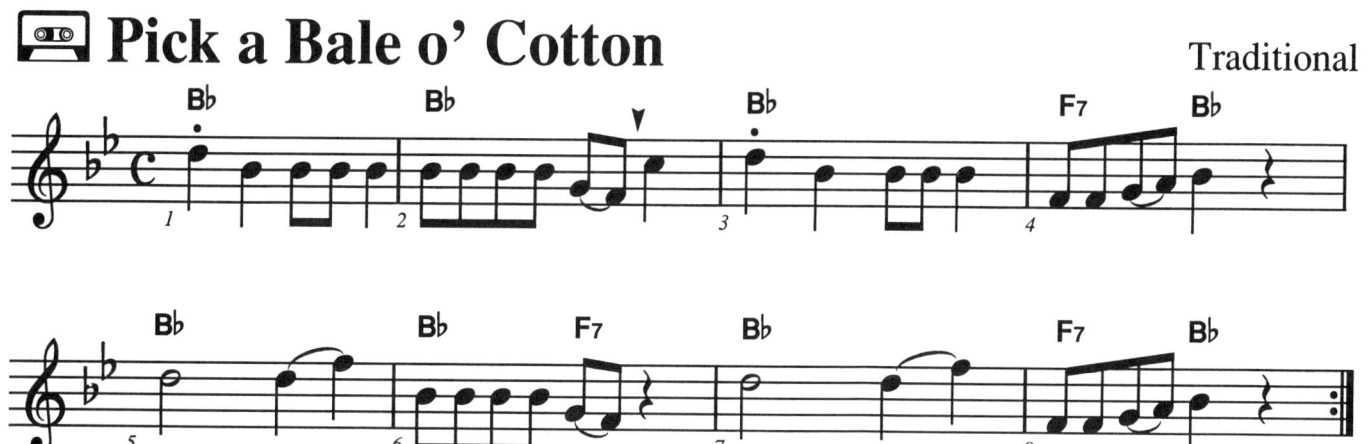

50

# 📼 The William Tell Overture

Giaocomo Rossini

On the cassette there are **three** drumbeats to introduce this song.

# 📼 Mexican Dance

Traditional

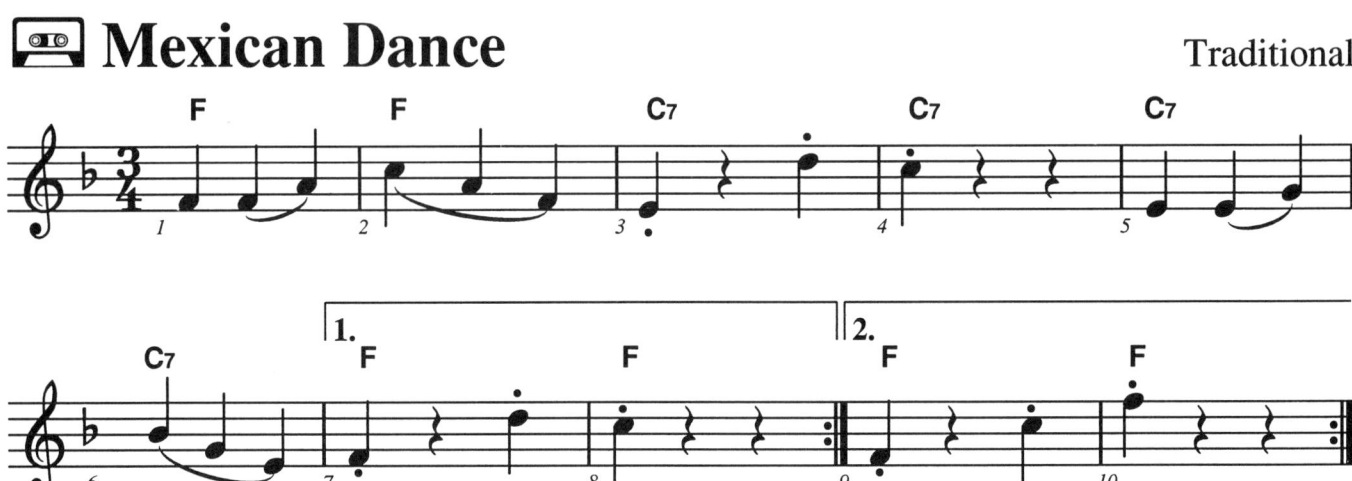

# 📼 Lavender's Blue

Traditional English

# 🎛 O Them Golden Slippers

J. A. Bland

# 🎛 Dance of the Hours

A. Poinchelli

On the cassette there are **three** drumbeats to introduce this song.

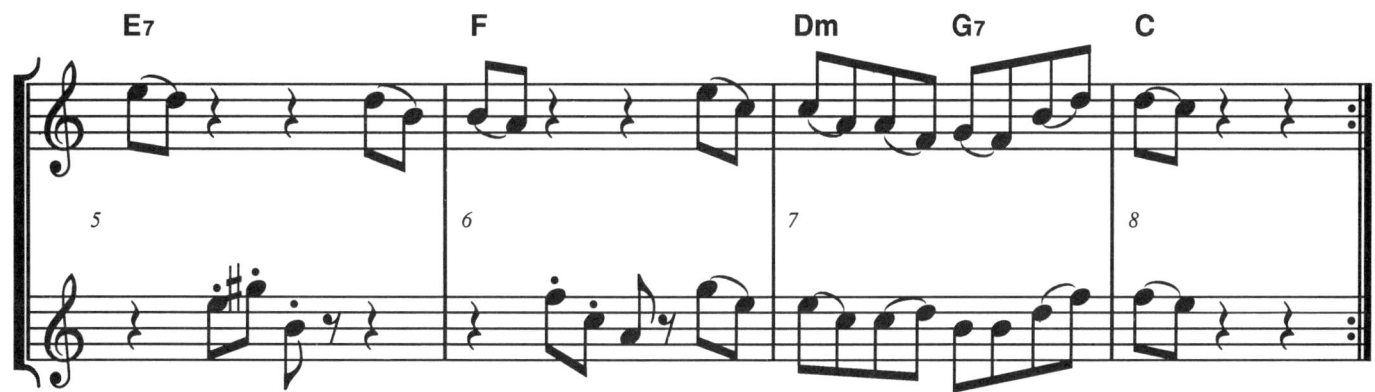

# Camptown Races

Stephen Foster

# Muss i Den

Traditional German

On the cassette there are **six** drumbeats to introduce this song.

# 📼 The Can-Can (Part 1)

Jacques Offenbach

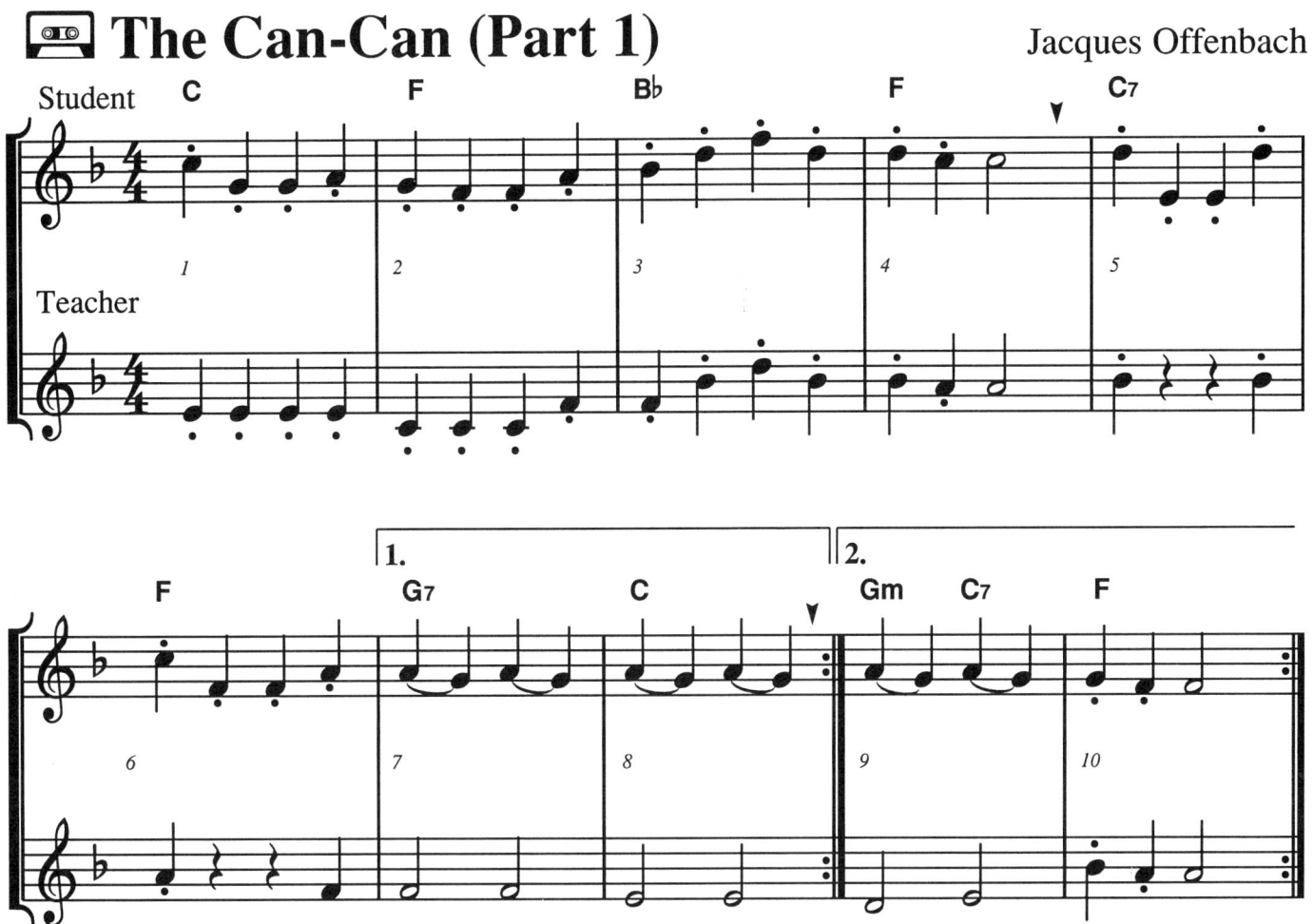

# Developing a Good Tone

The best way to develop a good tone on the flute is by consistent practice over a long period of time. The flute does not have a good tone built into it, like the piano. Consequently, effort is needed to make each note sound good, and in tune.

Always begin each practice session by warming up with a few exercises from previous lessons. Stop playing and let your lips rest if your tone becomes breathy or if your muscles won't respond. Your sound will have improved next time you pick up the instrument.

# Lesson 16
## The Note Low C

This is the lowest note on the flute. It corresponds to Middle C on the piano.

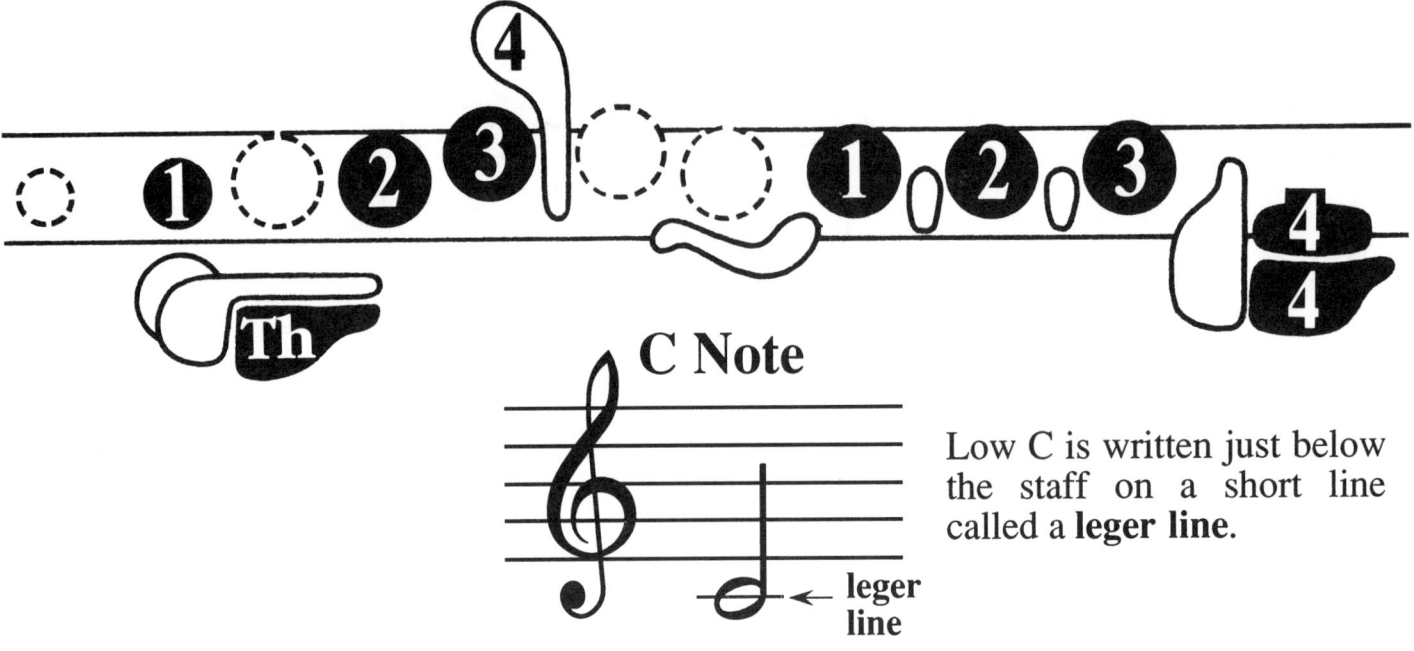

### C Note

Low C is written just below the staff on a short line called a **leger line**.

← leger line

## 📼 Exercise 36

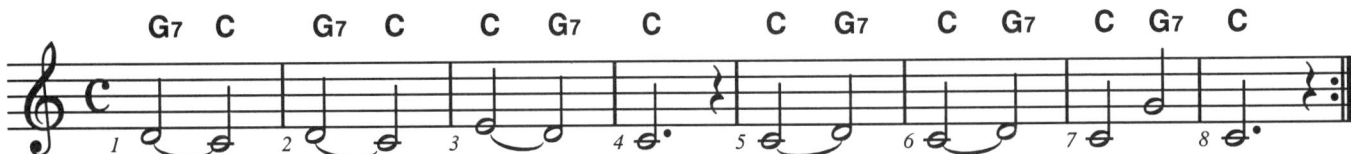

## 📼 God Rest Ye Merry Gentlemen

Traditional

On the cassette there are **three** drumbeats to introduce this song.

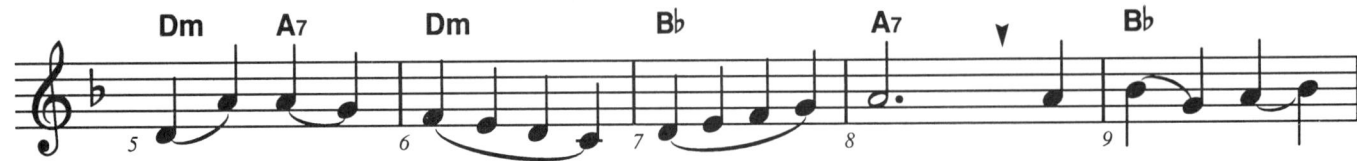

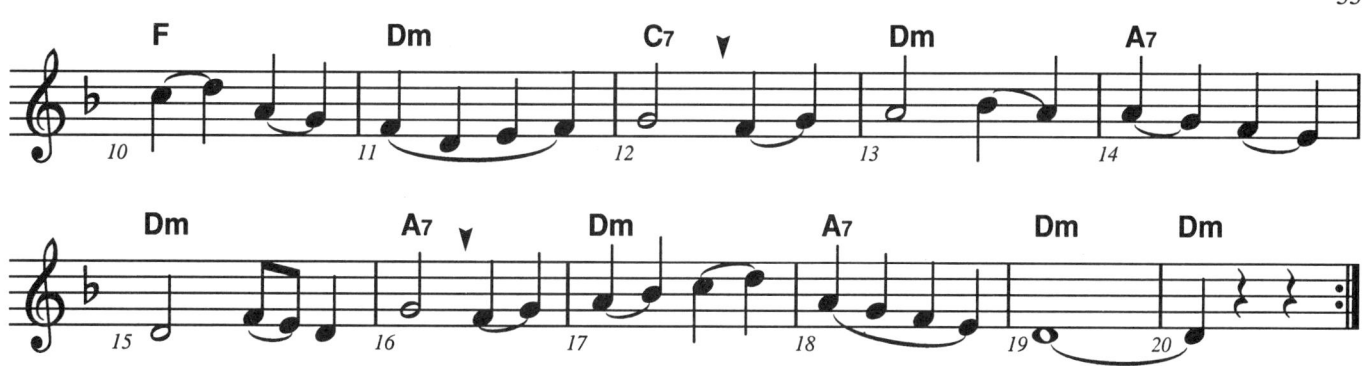

# The C Major Scale

A Major scale is a group of eight notes that produces the familiar sound:

**Do   Re   Mi   Fa   So   La   Ti   Do**

You now know enough notes to play the C Major scale:

**C     D     E     F     G     A     B     C**

## 🎴 Exercise 37

The number underneath each note indicates its position in the scale.

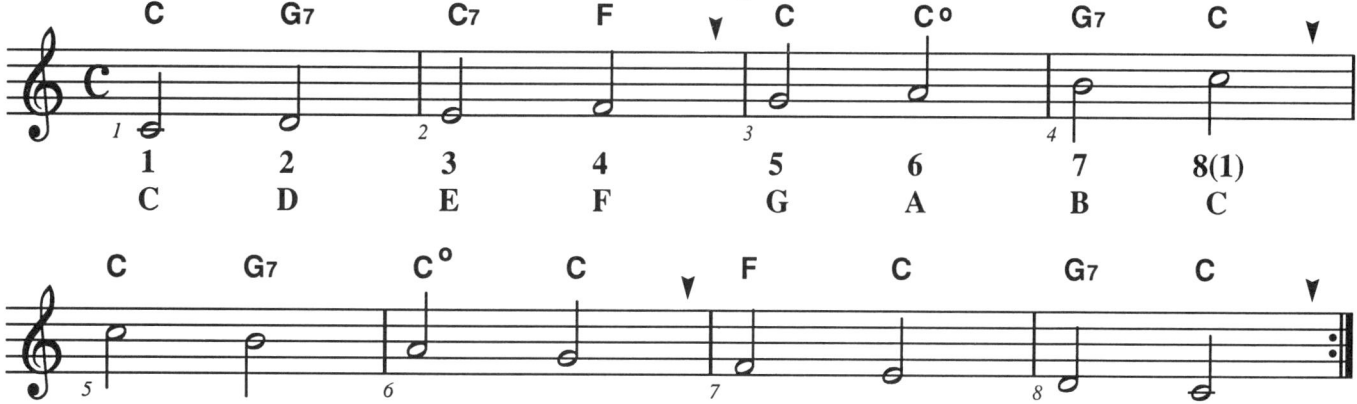

# The Octave

An **octave** is the interval of eight notes of a **Major scale**. The **first** note and the **last** note of a Major scale always have the same name. In the C Major scale the distance from Middle C to the C note above it (or from that C note down to Middle C) is one octave (eight notes).

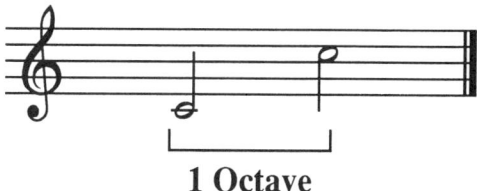

1 Octave

# Arpeggios

An **arpeggio** is the notes of a **chord** played one at a time. A chord is any three or more notes played together. Although you can't play chords on the flute you can play the notes of a chord one at a time; that is, you play arpeggios.

A Major arpeggio is constructed from the **first**, **third** and **fifth** notes of a Major scale.

The C Major arpeggio uses the 1st, 3rd and 5th notes from the C Major scale - **C**, **E** and **G**. When you play a C Major arpeggio, you are playing the notes of a C chord.

## 📼 Exercise 38     C Major Arpeggio

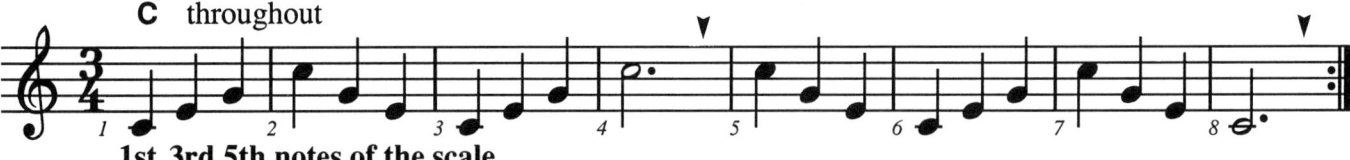

# The F Major Scale

## 📼 Exercise 39     The F Major Scale

The F Major scale contains one flat note - B♭.

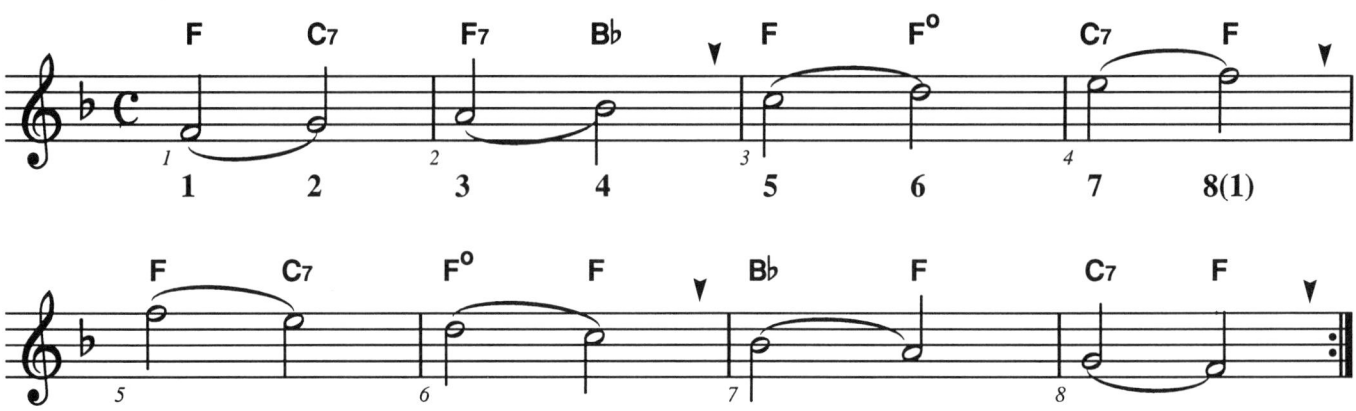

# F Major Arpeggio

You have seen that the C Major chord contains the first, third and fifth notes from the C Major scale, and that you could play a C Major arpeggio by playing the notes from that chord. The first, third and fifth notes from the F Major scale (F, A and C), when played together form the F chord. When you play them individually, these notes become an F arpeggio. When referring to a Major chord or arpeggio it is not always necessary to use the word "Major". "F arpeggio" means the F Major arpeggio, "C chord" means the C Major chord, and so on.

## 📼 Exercise 40

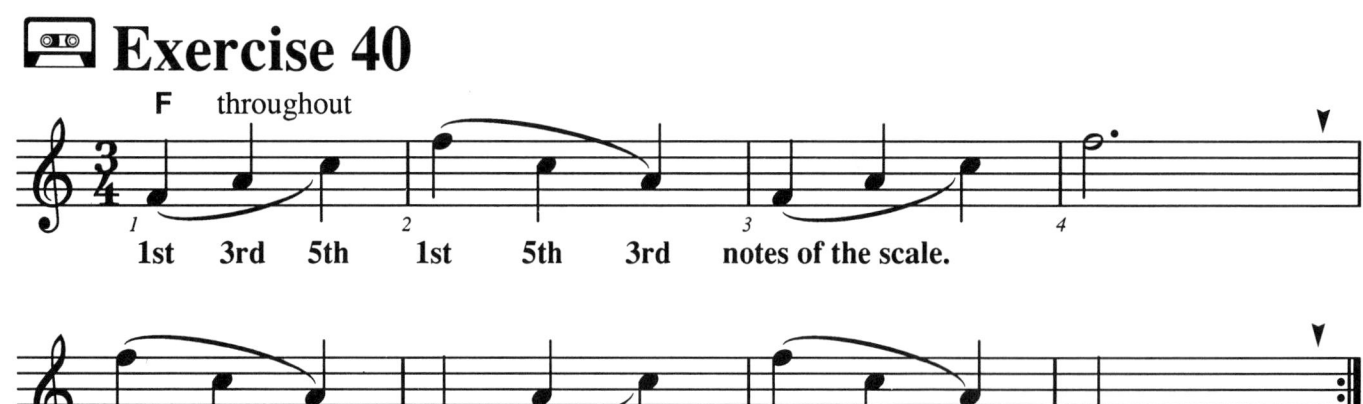

# Keys

When a song consists of notes from a particular scale, it is said to be written in the **key** which has the same name as that scale. For example, if a song contains mostly notes from the C Major scale, it is said to be in the key of C Major.

# Key Signatures

The number of sharp or flat signs after the treble clef is called the **key signature**. The key signature tells you which scale a melody is based on. So far you have played songs with several different key signatures, Eg:

**Key of C Major - no sharps or flats**

**Key of F Major - one flat (B♭)**

**Key of G Major - one sharp (F♯)**

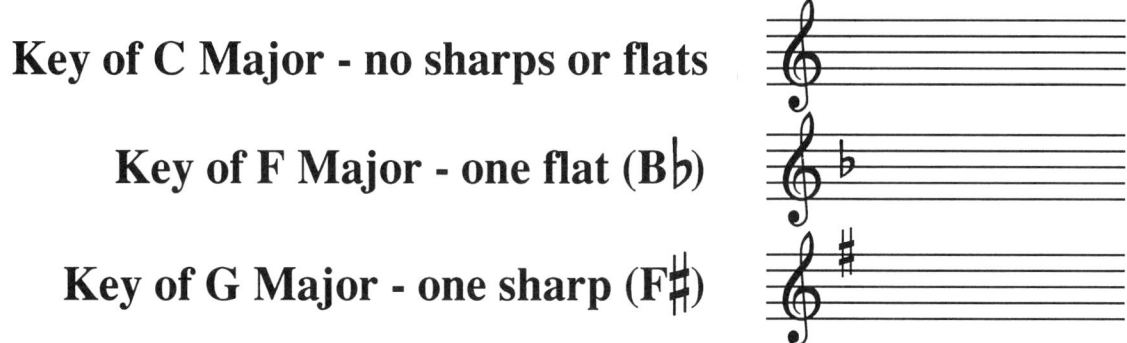

There are many other key signatures based on Major scales that you have not yet learnt. For more information on scales and keys, see Progressive Music Theory.

## The Caissons Go Rolling Along

Traditional

This song is written in the key of C Major.
On the cassette there are **six** drumbeats to introduce this song.

# 📼 The Can-Can (Part 2)

Jacques Offenbach

This song is written in the key of F Major.

Play all quarter notes staccato.

# Lesson 17
## The Note G in the Middle Register

The fingering for this note is the same as for G in the low register.

**G Note**

This G note is written in the **first** space above the staff.

Don't be dismayed if the note drops suddenly to the low register, or if it is very hard to start. The higher you play, the more demands you are making on your mouth. The secret lies in building up strength in your lip muscles. The more you practice the faster this will happen.

## Exercise 41

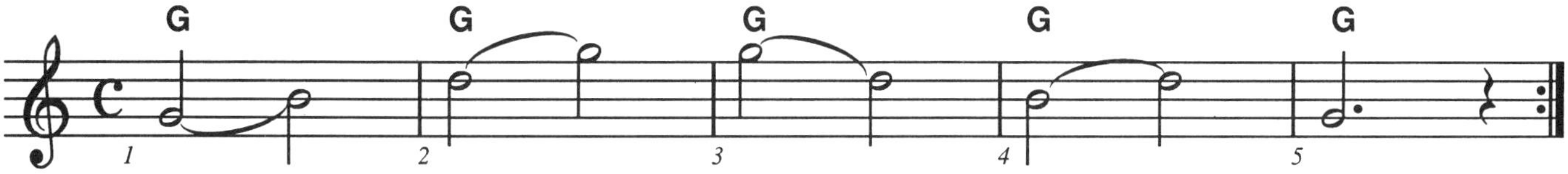

## Morning Has Broken

Traditional Scottish

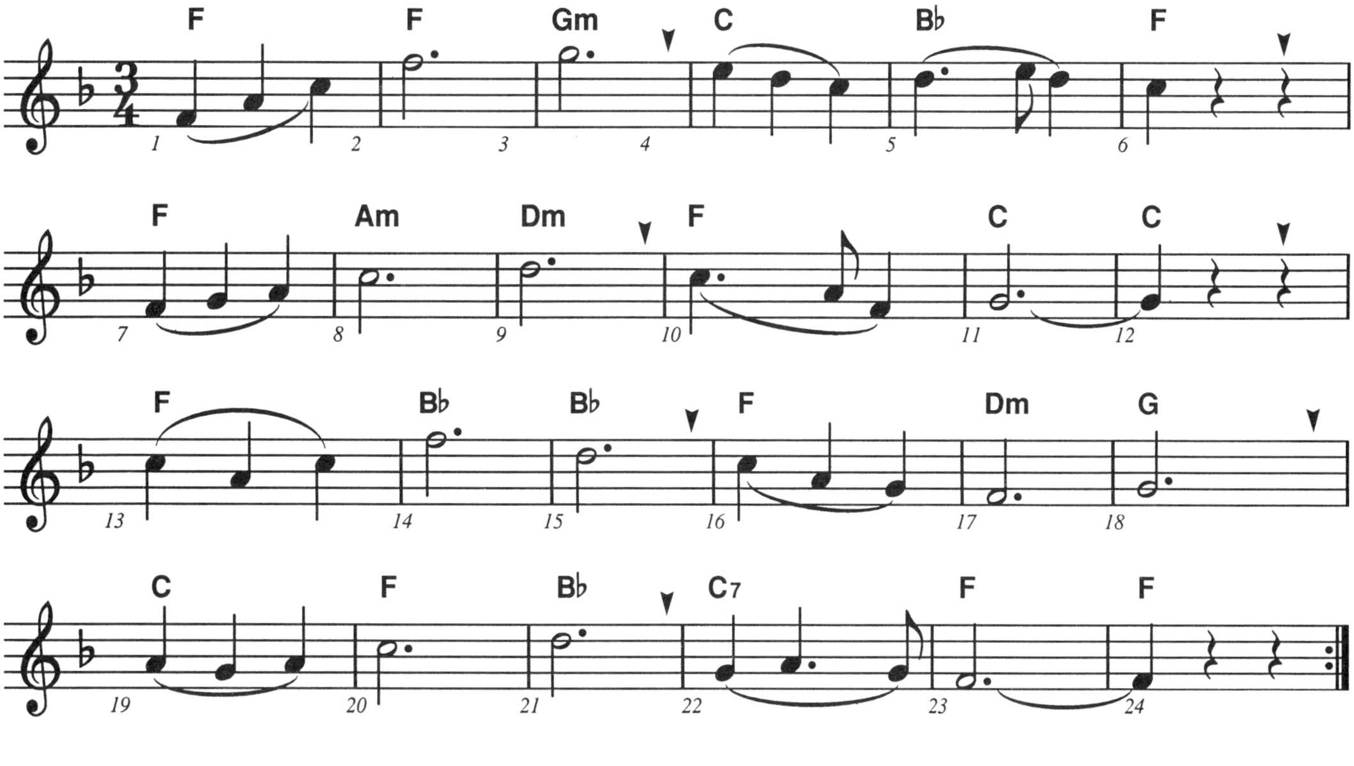

## 📼 Scarborough Fair

Traditional

## 📼 What Shall We Do With the Drunken Sailor?

Traditional

# Accidentals

When a sharp or flat sign is written immediately before a note, and is not part of a key signature, the sign is called an **accidental**. E.g. the sharp sign in bars 4, 15 and 38 of Beautiful Dreamer is an accidental because the note F♯ is not part of the F Major key signature.

## 📼 Beautiful Dreamer

Stephen Foster

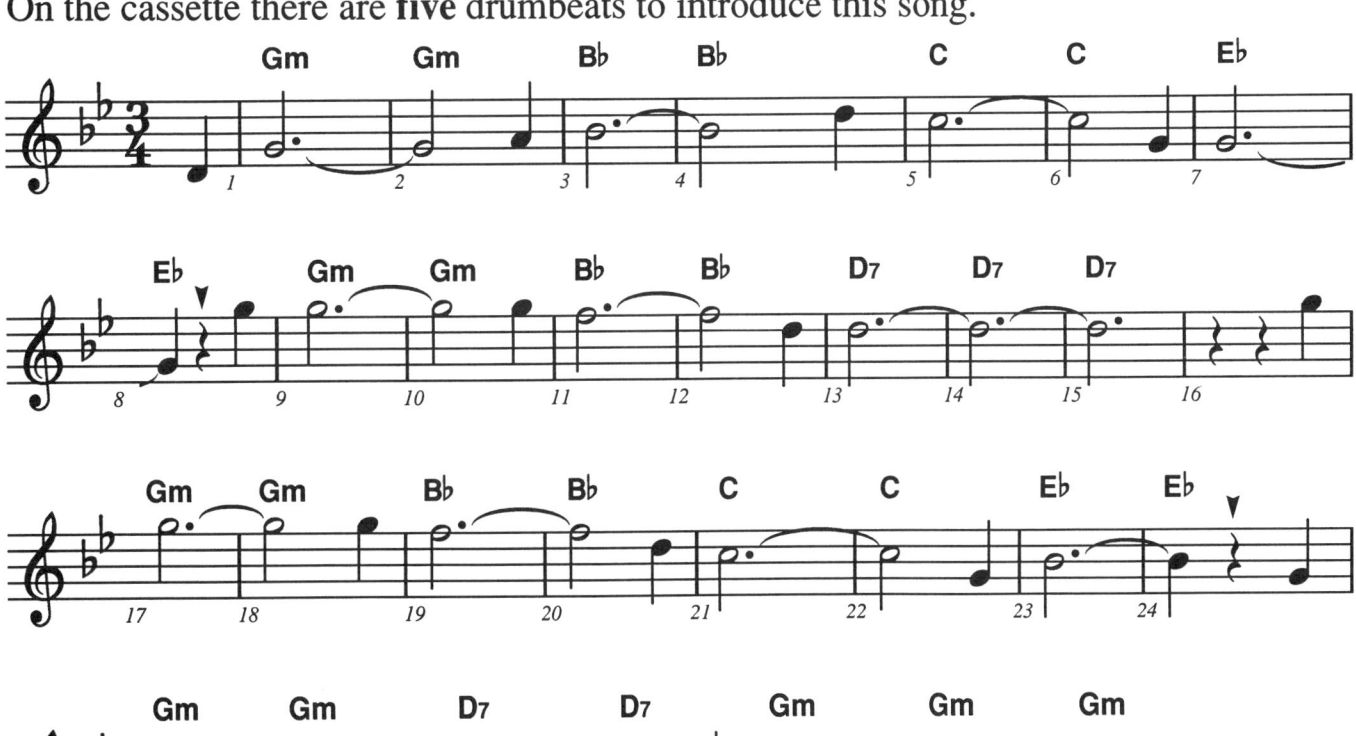

## 📼 House of the Rising Sun

Traditional

On the cassette there are **five** drumbeats to introduce this song.

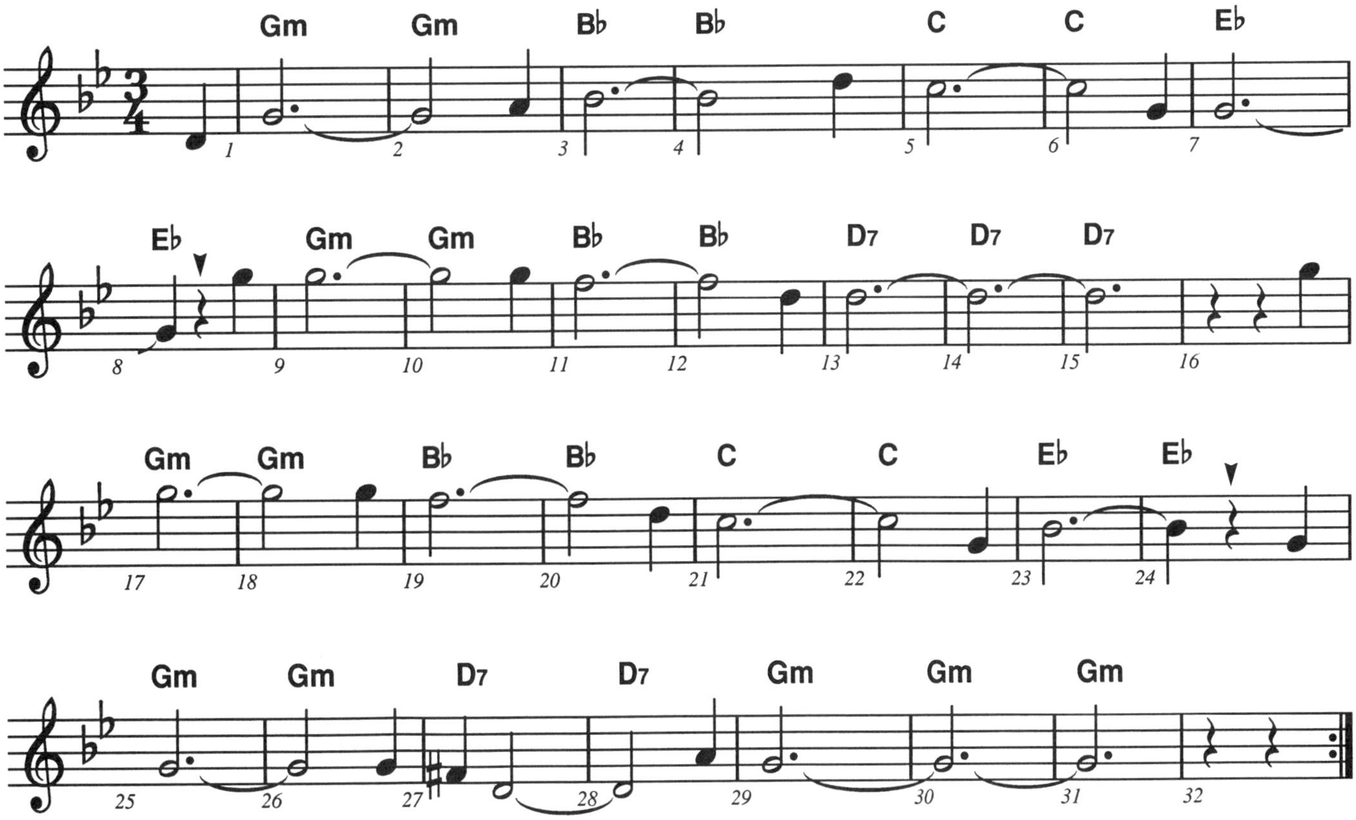

# Lesson 18
## The Note F♯ in the Middle Register

F♯ Note

The fingering for this note is the same as for F♯ in the low register.

## 🔊 Exercise 42

The sharp sign after the treble clef applies to F notes in both the low and the middle registers.

## 🔊 Serenade in G

Johannes S. Bach

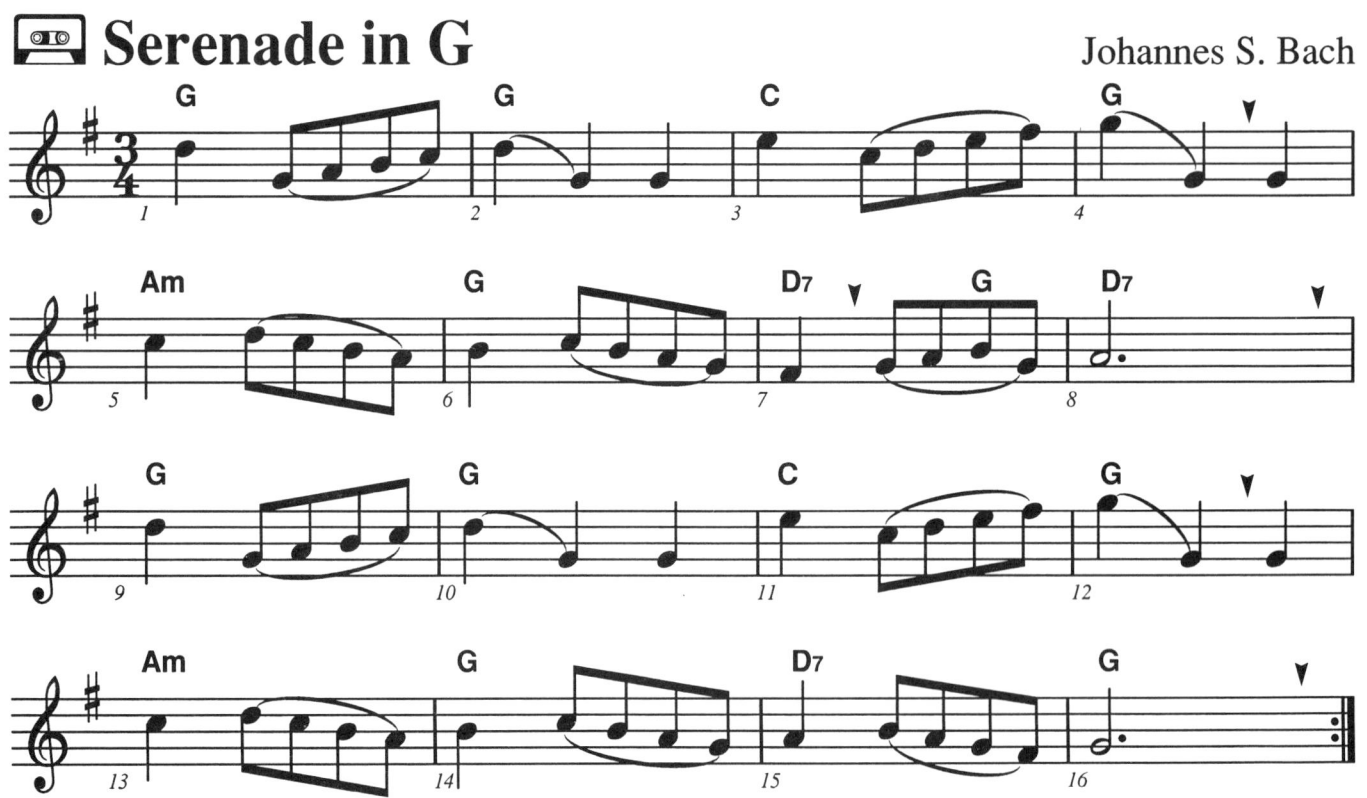

# 🎞 Sakura

Traditional Japanese

# 🎞 Lullaby

Johannes Brahms

On the cassette there are **five** drumbeats to introduce this song.

# Lesson 19
## The Natural Sign

 This is a natural sign. A natural sign cancels the effect of a sharp or a flat. E.g. Rock Riff 2 has the F Major key signature, which tells you to play all B notes as B♭. However, in bars 1, 2 and 3 there is a natural sign before the last B note in each bar. This natural sign cancels the effect of the key signature, and means that you play these notes as B instead of B♭.

## 🖭 Rock Riff 2

You may wish to use the alternate B♭ fingering (shown in the fingering index) for this piece.

## 🖭 Creepy Blues

The natural signs in front of the C notes in bars 2, 9 and 14 cancel the effect of the second sharp in the key signature, and indicate that you play those notes as C notes.

# The Note G♯

G♯ is the note in between A and G. This note is also known as A♭.

G♯ Note

## 🎞 Blues Scale

This is a commonly used scale in blues melodies.

## 🎞 Hello My Baby

Traditional

# Won't You Come Home, Bill Bailey

Hughie Cannon

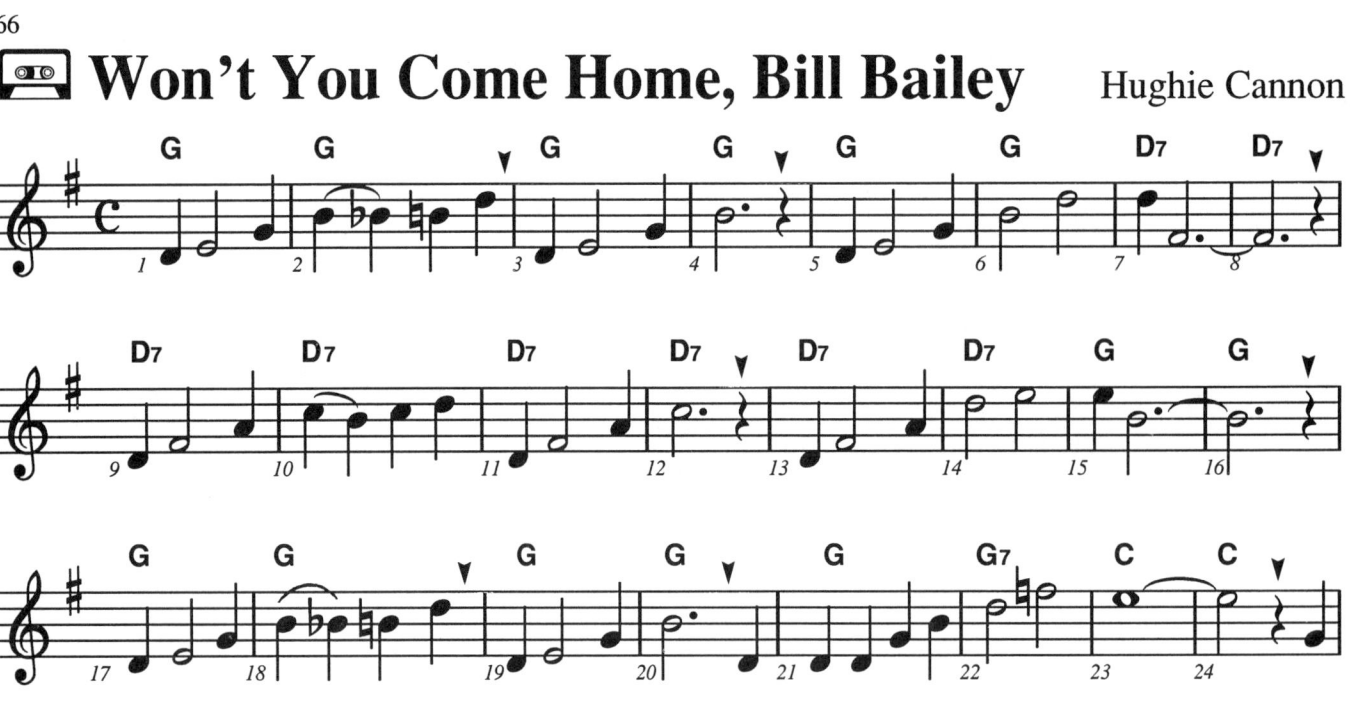

# Greensleeves

Traditional

Beware! In bars 14 and 30, the last note is G♯.
On the cassette there are **five** drumbeats to introduce this song.

# Index to Fingering

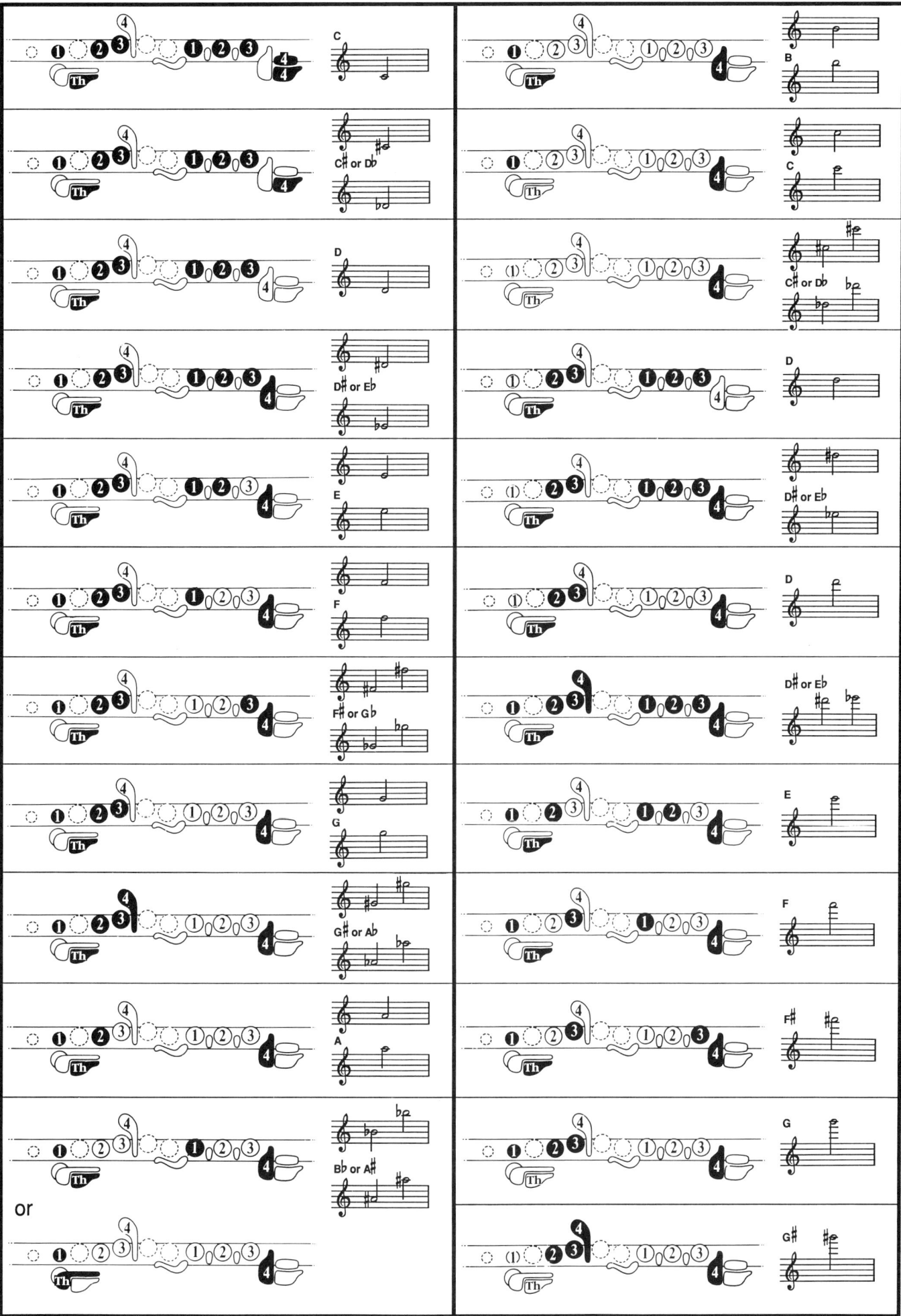

# Glossary of Musical Terms

**Accidental** - a sign used to show a temporary change in pitch of a note (e.g. sharp (#), flat (♭), double sharp (𝄪), double flat (𝄫), or natural (♮). The sharps or flats in a key signature are not regarded as accidentals.

**Arpeggio** - the playing of a chord in single note fashion.

**Augmented** - term usually applied to the fifth note of a scale or chord and which means that the fifth is raised by one semitone.

**Blues Scale** - consists of the 1st, ♭3rd, 4th, ♭5th, 5th and ♭7th notes of a major scale.

**Chord** - a combination of three or more different notes played together.

**Chromatic Scale** - a scale ascending and descending in semitones. e.g. C chromatic scale:

ascending: C C# D D# E F F# G G# A A# B C
descending: C B B♭ A A♭ G G♭ F E E♭ D D♭ C

**Diminished** - term usually applied to the fifth note of a scale or chord and which means that the fifth is lowered by one semitone.

**Double Flat** - a sign (𝄫) which lowers the pitch of a note by one tone.

**Double Sharp** - a sign (𝄪) which raises the pitch of a note by one tone.

**Embouchure** - A French word that means the position of the lips when playing a wind or brass instrument.

**Enharmonic** - describes the difference in notation, but not in pitch, of two notes, e.g.

F# or G♭

**Half Step** - same as semitone.

**Harmonic Minor Scale** - type of minor scale which is produced by flattening the third and sixth notes of a major scale. E.g., the C Harmonic Minor scale - C, D, E♭, F, G, A♭, B, C - is the C Major scale with its third and sixth notes flattened.

**Harmony** - the simultaneous sounding of two or more different notes.

**Improvise** - to perform spontaneously: i.e. not from memory or from a written copy.

**Interval** - the distance between any two notes of different pitches.

**Intonation** - the art of making each note perfectly in tune.

**Key** - describes the notes used in a composition in regards to the major or minor scale from which they are taken: e.g. a piece "in the key of C major" describes the melody, chords, etc. as predominantly consisting of the notes C, D, E, F, G, A and B - i.e. from the C scale.

**Keynote** - same as tonic, the note after which the key of a piece is named. E.g. in the key of F, the keynote is F.

**Key Signature** - a sign, placed at the beginning of each stave of music, directly after the clef, to indicate the key of a piece. The sign consists of a certain number of sharps or flats, which represent the sharps or flats found in the scale of the piece's key:
E.g.

indicates a scale with F# and C#, which is D major or B minor.

**Metronome** - a device which indicates the number of beats per minute, and which can be adjusted in accordance to the desired tempo.
e.g. **MM** (Maelzel Metronome) ♩ = 60 - indicates 60 quarter note beats per minute.

**Modulation** - the changing of key within a song (or chord progression).

**Natural Minor Scale** - the most useful type of minor scale. Produced by flattening the third, sixth and seventh notes of a major scale. E.g., the C Natural Minor scale - C, D, E♭, F, G, A♭, B♭, C - is the C Major scale with flat third, flat sixth, and flat seventh notes.

**Octave** - the distance between any given note with a set frequency, and another note with exactly double or half that frequency. Both notes will have the same letter name: e.g.

A440          A880

1 Octave

**Riff** - a pattern of notes that is repeated throughout a song.

**Semitone** - the smallest interval used in western music.

**Sixteenth Note** - a note with the value of a quarter of a beat in ⁴₄ time, indicated thus, ♬ (also called a semiquaver). The sixteenth rest, indicating a quarter of a beat of silence, is written: 𝄿

**Syncopation** - the placing of an accent on a normally unaccented beat: e.g.

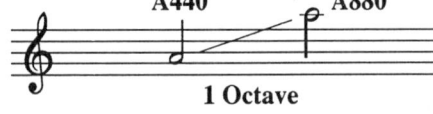

$\frac{4}{4}$  1  2  3  4          $\frac{3}{4}$  1 + 2 + 3 +

**Tempo** - the speed of a piece.

**Transposition** - the process of changing from one key to another.

**Unison** - to sing or play in unison - to sing or play the same notes.

**Vibrato** - subtle fluctuations in a note's pitch, adding expression to long notes.

**Whole Step** - same as whole tone, i.e., two semitones.